"Wouldn't more of our students love to be part of an authentic writing project like Wrinkles Wallace? Bravo to Mr. Parks for his voice and his example! He not only taught his students the elements of writing—he walked his talk."

—KIM OVERTON,
PRINCIPAL/TEACHER

"WWKNS is a rarity, a cliché-demolishing, guffaw-out-loud, 5280 feet-a-minute ride."

—DANIELLE BIRDYSHAW,
LITERACY COACH

"Wrinkles Wallace is a hit! By combining humor with a focus on impacting the lives of young people, this book is a must read for all young people. In fact, it's a must read for all those who care about children and their education."

—ROBERT W. SIMMONS III,
PROFESSOR, LOYOLA UNIVERSITY MARYLAND

WRINKLES WALLACE

Knights of Night School

TO: ETHAM
ENJOY!

By Marquin Parks

MERIDIA PUBLISHERS

ISBN: 978-0-9832330-5-3

This book is produced by Meridia Publishers with the collaboration of Dynasty Effect, LLC.

This book is a work of fiction. Any similarity to actual persons, living or dead, or institutions or other entities, is purely coincidental.

Inquiries should be directed to the Publishers at:
admin@meridiapublishers.com

Cover design by Peter Moffat www.rooted-design.co.uk
Typesetting by www.wordzworth.com
Printed in the United States of America

www.meridiapublishers.com

DEDICATED TO

My loving family and friends

and

My 4th/5th grade class of 2006-2007, Room 222.

Contents

I got a letter from the mailman the other day.

I opened and read it.

It said I failed 5th Grade.

CHAPTER 1

The Introduction

I figured it would be like that. I'd only known them for about fifteen minutes, but I knew it. Maybe my nerves were tingling. Maybe it was the Sour Boppers candy and Jumperz energy drink mixed into my pancakes that Grandma Wilbur cooked for breakfast. Nevertheless, my mind was racing and I was crazier than two galloping goats on a shopping spree. Oh, and by the way, my name is Wrinkles Wallace.

This morning was my first day at a new school. I was the newest student at Old Endings Preparatory in Ypsilanti, Michigan. If you have ever been to Ypsilanti, you would know about Old Endings Preparatory. It's the one and only blue building with vibrant yellow polka-dots in town. The rest of the buildings are comprised of painted stripes, plaids, and argyles. Needless to say, our polka-dots stick out. It's also safe to say, once you arrive at Old Endings Preparatory, doggone it, you know you've arrived.

My Grandma Wilbur dropped me off at school on her motorcycle and I tried to smoothly walk up the pathway. I only fell one time, which was a record low for me. I thought I showed my skills. However, my new school mates didn't recognize the talent. Some kid about the size of a baby Brontosaurus had the nerve to yell out, "Hey, clumsy!"

"No. That's my baby sister's name," I said.

"Your baby sister's name is Clumsy?" asked the kid.

"Yeah, and my name is Wrinkles. You must be Tiny. It's a pleasure to meet you." I extended my hand and quickly retracted it after I realized that his hands were covered in chocolate syrup. I gave him a friendly peace sign.

"How did you know my name?" asked Tiny, after licking some chocolate covered sprinkles off his left pinky. I shrugged my shoulders and headed into the building.

CHAPTER 2

The Entrance

I figured it would be like that. There were six bubble gum machines all along the wall. The gumballs in each machine seemed to grow in size. The first one had small marble-sized gumballs. The sixth one had gumballs that would last my whole life. I was tempted to get one, but I wasn't sure how my teacher would feel about me chewing gum in class. You know how some teachers think chewing gum in their classroom is somehow against some sort of law. Either you have to hide your gum and not enjoy chewing it, or you have to chew while they're not looking and risk biting your tongue. With my luck, I'd probably have to throw out my gum before the flavor was gone because my new teacher would ask me to stick out my colored tongue with the chewy gum on top.

In front of the bubble gum machines, located right in the middle of the hallway, was a raggedy quarter horse that you might find at a grocery store. Maybe I was guessing it was a quarter horse because all anyone could ride was the saddle on where the ribs of the horse might be. The rest of the horse's face and tail area were missing. The price for riding the horse was only twenty-five pennies, but you had to put each copper coin in one at a time.

For some reason, I could never pass up a chance to ride one of those horses at the grocery store. To me, it never got old, so I waited in line behind what looked to be a small group of kindergarteners. I could tell they were kindergarteners because everybody knows that kindergarten lines are blobs of human gigglers, poking and pushing each other.

Even though I couldn't see the action on the horse, about every thirty seconds I would hear a loud thud and a kindergartener would get up off the ground after being thrown off the rowdy quarter horse. The way those kindergarteners were being tossed, I ended up at the head of the blob in no time. The bell rang as I finished putting my shiny Abe Lincolns in the machine. I had just wasted 25 cents and it was time to go to class.

Ropes instantly fell from the ceiling. There were teachers standing above us yelling, "Get to class before the tardy bell rings!"

I figured it would be like that. I climbed the ropes like a human squirrel. Those who decided they would rather be tardy were in for a rude awakening. Another bell rang and the floor started to slowly separate. The ground began shaking like we were having a rumbling earthquake. A door below me opened, and the next thing I knew, I heard a lion roaring. Terrified screams filled the hallway. Instead of looking down to see what was about to happen, like most people would have, I kept climbing.

Finally, I made it.

CHAPTER 3

The Classroom

As you probably guessed by now, I figured the classroom would be like that. Yeah, it was typical. The mailboxes were along the side of the wall where mailboxes usually are. I remember calling those same mailboxes "cubbies" when I was in kindergarten, but around here, they were mailboxes. The white board was on the wall where white boards usually are. Everybody knows you don't put the white boards on the floor or ceiling. Although, writing on the floor would be pretty cool. One look up let me know that the ceiling tiles had probably been the victim of a horrific pencil explosion. There were holes in all of the tiles, but the pencils were missing.

It didn't take long for me to figure out where the bathroom was in the classroom. There was a green sign on the front of the door that meant it was okay to go in and handle your business. The only real problem I could see with using the bathroom was the fact that it was one of those portable bathrooms that you have to use at the carnival. You know, the type of bathroom that has those plastic walls and rocks from side to side when you step inside. Yeah, the one that when you're inside it, you can hear exactly what the people waiting in line are talking about. And, if you can hear them, they probably can hear you. I instantly knew I never wanted to use the bathroom in the classroom unless I happened to have an absolute emergency.

By the windows of the classroom was a small fish tank with four soft-shelled turtles. The lid to the tank had a lock with a spinning combination that you usually see on the end of a chain for a bike, or in a locker room. Someone had either put a lock on the tank to keep the turtles in, or keep people out.

Even though I probably should have gone straight to my seat, to sit down, I couldn't help but stop and look at what the turtles were doing. Their noses were making tiny sounds as they bumped them into the glass while they were trying to eat their food. Life for the four turtles had to be great since all they needed to do was swim around and eat shrimp. The only thing they were missing was a bowl of gravy. If they could somehow dunk those shrimp into some good ole' gravy, they'd be doin' it. I think gravy goes perfect with breakfast, lunch, dinner, dessert, and midnight snacks.

CHAPTER 4

The Teacher

It didn't take two hands to figure out that I was one of five folks in the class who wasn't the teacher. Our teacher looked like a normal elementary school teacher. The name written on the board let me know that I needed to call him Mr. Quiet. A closer look at the name tag on his desk let me know his mother and father actually named him Sittin' B. Quiet.

Mr. Quiet was the average age for a teacher. I could tell because his front two teeth were bigger than the other teeth and he was missing a few molars. He looked freshly shaven and had no facial hair, although his sideburns looked to be desperately trying to make it past his ears. He walked with a funky rhythm that told me he was indeed trying too hard to be cool for his age. His tennis shoes were black, covered with a layer of kickball field dust, and the laces were tattered on the ends.

When I finally settled into my desk, I heard someone in the class mumbling about Mr. Quiet not being good enough to be a teacher. I wasn't buying any of that talk because I've had teachers like Mr. Quiet before and I learned a lot from them. Teachers like Mr. Quiet are absolutely the smartest people in the world. They know how smart they are and they are willing to mumble about it under their breath on special occasions. If I had to guess how old Mr. Quiet was, I'd say somewhere between nine and eleven years old.

Now, if you've never had a teacher who was younger than you, then there is one thing you need to understand.

1. Knowledge has no height requirement.

CHAPTER 5

The Me

By now, I guess you might want to know more about me and why I'm the newest student at Old Endings Preparatory. Well, I thought I passed fifth grade, but, actually I failed because I missed too many homework assignments. Yeah, I failed fifth grade because I didn't do enough homework.

To be honest with you, it wasn't that I didn't do my homework; it was more that I didn't turn it in. Dirty dittos were balled up in my backpack or placed at the bottom of the recycle bin. They never seemed to make it into the "In Box" on my teacher's desk. Plus, I did have a little, tiny, miniscule problem with lying to my grandma about not having any homework, so I could go outside and play, watch television, and play video games.

I'd also had a slight habit of bending the truth around the corner on my teacher so situations would work in my favor. Let's just say I had a gift for story-telling, not to mention, it did feel good being smarter than the adults in my life. While I ended up pulling some fast ones on them at the time, it did come back to bite me on the backside. Maybe my little fibbing problem was a lot bigger than I thought.

I guess that's the reason why I'm at Old Endings Preparatory from now until the end of the year. Hopefully things go right this time around, because if I have to do fifth grade three times, I don't know what I'll do with myself. I mean, I'm 28 years old, and well, you know what that means.

CHAPTER 6

The Dragon

If you've ever been a student, I'm sure you know about a teacher's hearing. Some of them hear much better than dogs listening for a doorbell. It almost goes without saying that somebody with the last name "Quiet" would be a good judge of sound. As you probably guessed, Mr. Quiet was an expert at listening.

While I was sitting there waiting for class to start, I heard a sound that wasn't coming from the air conditioning unit, the turtle tank filter, or that annoying hum made by the lights in the ceiling. The noise actually was the whispers of a person in the class. Just looking at Mr. Quiet let me know I wasn't the only one who heard the talking. The problem was, Mr. Quiet had no clue as to who it was, but he looked like he wasn't the type of teacher who would rest until he had a confession from one of us.

And, as you can guess, I'm the type of person who seems to have an antenna of guilt super-glued to my forehead.

Mr. Quiet said, "Well, if it isn't Wrinkles Wallace."

"Yes. I am Wrinkles," I said.

"I've read through your files and I can see that you were probably the one who was running his gum chewers."

"Nope, that was not me. The only gum in my mouth is —"

Mr. Quiet interrupted me and said, "Cut the cheese, Wrinkles. I know all about you because my aunt went to school with you. She told me all about how you and your friends would crack jokes and treat her badly. You called her 'Bowling Ball' because of how round she was. I know all about your evil ways. With that being said, Wrinkles, by the time I count to ten you need to be at my desk. One, two, four…"

As I lunged out of my desk, fell, jumped back up, and moved toward Mr. Quiet, my mind was in reverse and my past was coming back to haunt me again. Yeah, the girl was round, but who knew Susie "Bowling Ball" Paul would remember my little bowling ball joke for the rest of her life? Who knew her nephew would be my fifth grade teacher? I mean, it was a joke and we all laughed at her. Plus, Susie never complained about it at the time.

I even remember when our teacher took attendance. She would be calling out names, and when she got to Susie's, she'd pause just long enough for us to slip "Bowling Ball" in between Susie's first and last name. The teacher would try to keep a straight face and we'd all get the giggles. I still think the teacher was in on the joke.

Three seconds later I was at Mr. Quiet's desk, but he had skipped a few numbers and was up to nine. He looked me in the eyes and smiled. I looked back and noticed his pupils were like fudge brownies with chocolate sauce. Or, maybe I just had chocolate on the brain. Mr. Quiet reached into the bottom drawer of his desk, which looked a lot like a junk food drawer you'd find in a kitchen, and pulled out a bag of nacho cheese chips. He opened the bag and pulled out a three-sided polygon of garlic death.

"Wrinkles, you should try one!" said Mr. Quiet.

Normally, I'm all for chips, except, I was still full from those Sour Boppers pancakes that Grandma Wilbur made me for breakfast.

"Thanks, but no thanks, Mr. Quiet."

"Mind if I have one?" asked Mr. Quiet.

I paused and thought for a second. Everybody knows the smell of nacho cheese chips is almost worse than cigarette smoke, but what could I say to him? Maybe he was hungry.

I replied, "Whatever tantalizes your taste buds, Mr. Quiet."

Mr. Quiet opened his mouth and started gnawing on the chip like a gerbil devours the cardboard on an empty roll of toilet paper. Small crumbs landed in the lap of his navy blue pants. He used his left index finger to pick up the leftovers. I could see right then that not much gets by this guy. Not a crumb. Not a sound. Nothing.

That's when Mr. Quiet surprised me. He smiled with the grin that makes most grandmothers melt and leaves students wondering if their teacher should be sent to the Crazy House. There was no reason for his smile. There was no reason for him to be in a good mood. Not after knowing that I had made fun of his aunt. Not after some nacho cheese chips. I mean, no nacho cheese chips in the entire world are that good. Not even the ones that Grandma Wilbur makes.

It didn't take long for me to realize that the smile Mr. Quiet gave included a major problem. His smile smelled like his breath. See, I was standing maybe two feet from Mr.

Quiet because I wanted to give him his personal space. I'm a big fan of personal space. That's when he used his left index finger to motion for me to come closer. I did. He motioned for me to come even closer. I did. He finally stopped exercising his left index finger when I was bent over enough to have my nose less than an inch from his mouth.

Oh my.

All I could smell was nacho cheese chips and my eyes could only see the decorations in Mr. Quiet's nostrils. Message to self: *When was the last time he had cleaned his nose?* He reminded me that mine was empty.

Mr. Quiet asked, "Why?"

Instantly, my nose hairs were set on fire. I felt the blast of breath that had to be one hundred degrees rushing out of Mr. Quiet's mouth. I wished he could wrap his mouth around the air conditioner that was in the kitchen window at Grandma Wilbur's house. I'd do anything to be able to breathe out of my toes. Smelling my own stinking feet had to be one million times better than smelling Mr. Quiet's words. I felt like I was on a seesaw. I was going down and the Sour Boppers pancakes were coming up. He grabbed my chin hairs and brought my face closer.

"Did you hear me?" he asked.

Each word felt like the scorching blast you get when trying to open the oven door while taking out a batch of burnt cookies. Believe me, he had the temperature set on broil and I wanted to die.

"Yes!" I replied.

Mr. Quiet blurted, "Weeeeellll, THen next TIme, anSSSweRRRR mEEE."

I tightened my lips with a flimsy attempt to cover up the

lower half of my nostrils. He quickly melted my feeble plan and proceeded to exhale two lungs full of steamy, stinking carbon dioxide. My eyes rolled into the back of my head. I was nearly out on my feet. I felt like the heavyweight champion of the world busted me in the nose with a glove full of concrete.

Mr. Quiet said, "WRRRRinKleSSSS, you SSSSaiD you DiDn'T MinD mEE eaTTinG. NoWW, TOOo TeacHH you REESPONSiBiLiTY (my heart nearly stopped after that word, but the gasp of my classmates kept me alive) FoRR YouRR ACTIONS, I'M GOING TO GIVE YOU A PROJECT."

By this time I was willing to do anything to get away from his dragon breath. I shook my head from side to side and said, "No problem, Mr. Quiet. Anything you say."

He reopened his junk food drawer and fished out a carton of eggs. Why he'd have a dozen eggs just living in his junk food drawer is beyond me. I mean, I can understand keeping the chips in there, but eggs, not so much. Eggs typically live in refrigerators, boiling water, frying pans, or even cake batter. Nobody with any sense would keep eggs in their desk drawer.

"Wrinkles, how many eggs are in a dozen?" asked Mr. Quiet.

I tried to use my breath to defend myself against his breath and I answered, "Twelve."

"Correct! But that doesn't mean you have twelve chances to get this right. You only have two chances each day. If both of your eggs are broken then you fail for the day. Wrinkles, you must take this egg with you everywhere you go. You must keep an egg with you for everything you do. If you are in the shower, shampoo the egg's head. If you go to the mall, the egg needs new clothes. You must take an egg with you, no matter what. There will be no egg babysitters. Your Grandma Wilbur, which, by the way, is an odd name for a woman, cannot babysit the egg. It is solely your responsibility. If I, or anybody else, see you without your egg, you will fail this class. Oh, and by the way, these are not hard-boiled. I have special stickers that I have put on your eggs. When you do break both eggs in a 24-hour period, which you will, you will fail. Do we have an understanding, Wrinkles?"

"Yes, Sir."

Mr. Quiet placed the first egg in my hand and pointed for me to go back to my desk. After I sat down, it took about five minutes before I extinguished the forest fire in my nose and regained full consciousness. When I finally did come to my senses I realized I was going to be in for some serious trouble. Those eggs were going to make me a fifth grader for life. As often as I fell, the egg would be scrambled and I'd be toast.

This whole situation wasn't fair at all. Who would talk, with nacho cheese breath, to a student? Who would make a student carry eggs to pass fifth grade? Mr. Quiet would, and if he knew I played dodgeball on Wednesday nights, I'm guessing he probably wouldn't have cared. All I could think was: How was I supposed to avoid making egg salad sandwiches during a dodgeball game?

CHAPTER 7

The Others

As I said before, there were four other people in the class-room who weren't the teacher. I could look and see we were all different. Shortly after Mr. Quiet finished with my nacho chip trip, he gave the others their assignments.

First, there was Lenny. Mr. Quiet sat him on the side of the classroom. Lenny had to be at least seventy years old. I couldn't figure out how he climbed up the rope and avoided the lion. One glance at his area instantly let me know he had been in this class before and my first day was not his first day.

From the way things looked, Lenny worked at the school as a teacher's aide or a volunteer grandparent. Then I started to think that he lived at Old Endings Preparatory. I mean, his mail even had the school's address on it. His miniature refrigerator, microwave, toaster oven, coffee pot, and television did suggest he was making himself at home. Lenny sat in his wheelchair with a crossword puzzle book on his lap. He almost looked too comfortable with being at school.

Lenny sported cream-colored no-tie shoes, and glasses that had a string attached to the arms so he would not lose them. Under his royal blue smock was a white, long-sleeved button-up that served as the background for his tie. The smock had "LENNY" stitched on the left pocket. Lenny's slacks were stopped suddenly at the middle of his shin and they helped show off the lower red and blue colors of his red, white, and blue tube socks.

Instead of hair, Lenny's head was wrapped in silver tree garland. The thinning garland turned his former forehead to at least a six-head in size. His neck had a gobbler that moved more often than the two nervous turkeys, waiting for a Thanksgiving Presidential Pardon.

Chances are you are wondering why Mr. Quiet would need Lenny to be a teacher's aide or one of those grandparents who come in and read to the kids. Well, hold that thought because Lenny wasn't Mr. Quiet's aide or grandparent. Actually, Lenny was also a fifth grader in the class. Yeah, it shocked me too. From what I gathered, Lenny needed a mouth muzzle to keep his wooden teeth clamped shut. He flunked etiquette in fifth grade. His scores were the worst in his entire generation and he had the nerve to sit there and be proud of it. He wasn't always like this though.

When Lenny was nine, his entire family started laughing at him for having some lettuce from lunch covering his front teeth. They didn't stop for two hours. Lenny managed to turn the tables by dinner time and made everyone cry. From then on he's been on a mission to make others feel how he felt.

Lenny interrupts, moans, groans, complains, calls out, clowns, distracts, and does anything he can to get on your last nerve. He's so good at it that sports teams used to pay him to sit behind the opposing team's bench and fling insults. The players couldn't perform under the pressure of Lenny's insults. Finally, every professional sporting league banned him from their buildings. In turn, he protested outside and made fun of the fans who were going in to see the games. Eventually he had to hire bodyguards to protect him. He was a yo' momma joking, you're so dumb, you have the brains of a, nana-nana boo-boo…, Wrinkles-Wrinkles-bo-binkles-banana-fanna…, ornery and mean for no reason, ring your doorbell a thousand times at six in the morning, just to wake you up out of some good drooling sleep type of person. He greets everybody with the phrase, "You suck. You're not good at anything!" Then, once he starts to really hurt your feelings, he'll say, "I'll stop if you cry." Of course I ignored him because I am good at some things and crying isn't a big deal to me. Lenny's assignment was to make it through one full school day without insulting anybody. Lenny would probably be a fifth grader for life.

Sitting in front of Lenny was a girl. Her name was Urhiness (or Your Minus, as Lenny called her). Her name sounded like somebody was rushing to call a royal woman, "Your Highness." She's eighteen years old and she was in the class to finish fifth grade because she wanted to go to college with her friends. Years ago, she used to be late or absent all the time because she could not get away from the mirror. She would wake up early and still get to school late because of all the time she spent trying on outfits and doing her hair. Even when her mother dropped her off on time, she would stop and look at herself in the mirror of some teacher's car or check her makeup in the reflection of one of the windows. Urhiness' teachers said she was tardy to the party. Her excuse was always, "My mirror made me do it." Really, all that *me* did was make Urhiness fashionably late for graduating 5th grade.

Urhiness' issues started when she was about four. She'd see billboards, movies, and lots of stuff on television that made her think looks had to be more important than anything else. Then she got some wacky magazine that didn't help. Those magazines only gave her more reason to think all that mattered were looks.

Urhiness sat in class wearing a cardboard crown covered in rhinestones. From the looks of it, she probably had that crown resting on her head every day. She wore a black leather jacket with spider webs sewn near the collar and a hot pink t-shirt underneath. The shirt had the words, "Boys Lie," in matching glitter. She wore loose-fitting blue jeans with holes ripped in both knees. Somebody wrote the words "left" and "right" on the wrong kneecaps. The lower part of her denim legs were cut into strips and the ends were in knots. From where I sat, it looked like she had mop heads on the bottom of her legs. When she made her flip-flopped feet hop up and down, the mop heads actually shined her toenails like a miniature carwash. I guess those were the styles that were coming over from the fashion runways.

Personally, if somebody tried to get me to wear pants like that, I'd run far away. Although, I'd love to try to talk my Grandma Wilbur into wearing pants and flip-flops like that, but her feet stink and she prefers her military-issued combat boots. Mr. Quiet told Urhiness that passing fifth grade meant not looking into a mirror and being concerned with her looks for a whole school day. Let's just say, even she can't see herself doing that.

Another classmate of mine was Spork (or Pork, as Lenny called her). Spork stood in the rear of the classroom in a kitchen-like area. Spork, age forty-five, wore a typical chef's outfit that included an extremely large white chef's hat with a variety of splatters on it. Spork's hair looked like pink cotton candy had been spun around her head. Her feet were like she baked stocking-frosted bread inside her shoes. Spork's little eyes looked like potato slices with steak sauce in the center, beneath black pepper eyebrows. Her mouth had teeth that were similar to candy corn attached to bubble gum looking gums. Her ears appeared to be made of fried jumbo shrimp and her fingers reminded me of slender breakfast sausages. Honestly, Spork's body actually looked like things you might find in your pantry and refrigerator.

Spork's so called "kitchen" was an overcrowded, hot mess. I thought a tornado had touched down in the area. Her hot plate, barbecue grill, electric skillet, turkey fryer, and Food Lovin' Oven were all plugged into the same outlet that was right below a sign written in dried barbeque sauce with the words, RESPECT MY SPATULA. Needless to say, her area would keep stop, drop, and rollers bruised and dizzy because it was a fire waiting to happen.

While Spork did have all of the proper equipment to run her own small restaurant, her cooking was absolutely hor-rterrible (combine horrible and terrible). She had already failed Culinary Arts (cooking class) in fifth grade over thirty years ago and had been trying to pass for the last five years. From what I could see and smell, you wouldn't catch me sampling anything she cooked because I wasn't into the garbage alfredo she would try to whip up. In order for Spork to pass, Mr. Quiet required that she make edible meals in school. Spork thinks the second she passes she'll open her own restaurant.

My final classmate was asleep the entire time. Seriously, he just sat there in his chair with his head down the *whole* time. His name was Snooze (yeah, Lenny called him Lose and Snooze U. Lose). He was about thirty, but I'm guessing because I really couldn't get a good look at his face.

Snooze wore a one-piece black pajama outfit with the crusty enclosed feet clinging for dear life. Covering his eyes was one of those sleeping masks that some people wear to keep light away from their eyes. The icing on Snooze's sleep cake was the fact that he would snore like a freight train. I mean, he made noises while he slept that words cannot describe. Some of them were half pig oink, half buzz saw, with a hint of seagull squawk.

If you could get over Snooze's constant snoring, his drooling would probably work your last nerve. Snooze drooled like nobody's business and his mouth dripped like a faucet. The slow drips of drops rolled off the lower left corner of his desk and landed in a pot with an amazingly loud plop about every five seconds or so. I don't know how he could continue to lose that much saliva and not be dehydrated. Every half hour Mr. Quiet would come over and replace the pot with an empty one. Then he would give the filled pot of saliva to Spork so she could try to make boiled water.

She couldn't.

Another Snooze-able issue (aside from the fact that he was a slip and fall hazard) was the fact that he talked in his sleep. During the middle of the morning lesson he rambled about things that made no sense whatsoever, yet the rambles did actually answer the questions Mr. Quiet asked us.

Snooze would blurt out things like, "I want a pile of peel!"

That was the answer to a question about what to do with old indoor food that you take outside.

When Mr. Quiet asked questions about things that described us, Snooze snored out, "I sleep, therefore I am."

It took us a while to figure out what he was saying and how it tied into the lesson, but when we did, it made his rambling easier to deal with. Snooze's assignment was to stay up for an entire school day. Needless to say, Snooze's bed bugs will be biting for quite some time.

Once Mr. Quiet gave us our assignments, he uttered the unthinkable. I could barely believe the words pouring out of his mouth as he said them.

Mr. Quiet said, "I know some of you have been here for a while, but today I'm pushing the reset button. Today is everyone's first day. Starting today, the day you pass is the day you walk out of this class. I'm not going to make any of you stay until the end of the year. If you can show me that you're over your issues, in one school day, then you're out of here. Urhiness, if you can make it without your mirror, see you later! Snooze, if you can stay awake, sayonara, snorer! Spork, if you can cook something that isn't gross, adios! Lenny, if your words are enough to make an alligator smile, in a while, crocodile! Wrinkles, if you can keep one of those eggs better than a waiter, I'll see you later!"

It took me a few minutes to fully understand that all I had to do was keep an egg for one school day and I would pass. It also meant that I was in a class full of people with issues. Where were the kids who didn't have problems turning in homework or being nice to people? Maybe they weren't the type of people who needed to go through fifth grade twice.

CHAPTER 8

The Ingredients

Have you ever been extremely tired in school? I mean, the stayed-up-late-watching-your-favorite-television-show type of tired that might have you dozing off into a trance. In my head, I was at this place where Grandma Wilbur and I eat chocolate covered Yummy Gummy Worms and drink spicy lemonade.

In the meantime, Spork had managed to ease over to my desk, swipe my egg, and replace it with a small squeezable globe. I guess something in her mind told her that she could pass the class if she played her cards right. The problem was, those cards just so happened to include using my egg. She returned to her area and began whizzing through her cookbooks and looking up recipes that included eggs. She finally decided to make a Shark Knuckle Omelet. No, no need to rub your eyes and reread. Spork really intended to make a Shark Knuckle Omelet.

Now, I have no clue what store on Earth sells shark knuckles. I've been to plenty of dollar stores. I've even been to many Free Whoopin' stores, but I've never walked into a store that sold shark knuckles. Plus, some sharks are on the endangered species list. They can bite you, but you cannot bite them.

Well, somewhere boiling in her brain, Spork found a substitute for the shark knuckle taste by blending together various spices, seaweed, and ocean-bottom mud to give it that pure, one-of-a-kind wild shark knuckle flavor. Instead of shark meat, she used a substance called tofu. I'm no chef on the Hungry Channel, but I think tofu takes on the taste of the ingredients you cook. If you were to use some chicken broth, then the tofu would taste like chicken. All in all, tofu reminds me of fancy instant noodles with a packet of special flavor, but I could be wrong.

Spork's only problem (besides not being able to cook) was finding the tofu to substitute for the actual shark knuckle. So, like any cook would do, she improvised. Spork took off her shoes and removed her socks. She grabbed a bowl and a small cheese grater from the cabinet under the sink. She began grating the dry skin off the bottom of her feet. She used a grapefruit spoon to get all the toe jam from between her toes. Then, she clipped her toenails and put them in the bowl. Voilà! She had homemade toe-food.

When Spork finished adding her ingredients to the bowl, she realized that Mr. Quiet would need more ingredients to have a bigger portion. He'd probably want to get nice and full because with any excellent meal, people get greedy. To solve the ingredient issue, Spork walked over to Lenny to get some help. She told him he deserved a pedicure. He mumbled back something about his feet smelling as good as her last meal.

Spork ignored Lenny's words and unstrapped his shoes. She nearly tossed her cookies because Lenny's feet had the smell of alligator belly on them. She rolled his tube socks down to his ankles and was forced to stop. Somehow the socks wouldn't roll down anymore because they were too stiff and crusty. She grabbed an area where his toes should have been and pulled until the socks slowly came off.

From there, Spork emptied the contents of Lenny's socks into the bowl. He had two dollars and thirty-seven cents (which she kept as a tip), some mud, a feather, two marbles, and something that looked a lot like a big toe, or a dirty circus peanut. It was hard to tell because Spork counted five toes on Lenny's left foot and six on his right foot. She paused for a second, and realized if it was a real toe, she wasn't eating it anyway.

Though Spork had a lot of ingredients from Lenny's socks, she wasn't happy until she rubbed both of his socks together to get the crust off and into the bowl. The crust at the bottom of the socks started smoking and almost started a fire, before Spork realized something was about to burn.

Next, Spork proceeded to give Lenny a pedicure with the spoon and cheese grater. Somehow she came to the conclusion that Lenny's eleven toenails were far too long for her nail clippers to cut. That was no problem for Spork because she bit all eleven of his funky toenails off in no time. I guess she was really on a mission to pass the class and get that restaurant going.

CHAPTER 9

The Making

After Spork had the shark knuckle ingredients ready, she fired up the stove and took out a large crusty-bottomed cast iron skillet from the dirty dishwater. The nasty skillet still had old failing food on it from the last time she tried to cook something. Better Mr. Quiet eating Spork's entrées than me.

As the fire crackled from the water evaporating off the bottom of the skillet, Spork began reading the recipe's directions. The recipe called for butter or margarine to stop the egg from sticking to the surface of the skillet. Spork didn't have any margarine or butter, but she did have some lip balm. She used her index finger to scoop out the rest of the lip balm and flicked it into the skillet. She picked the skillet up by the handle and maneuvered it so the lip balm melted evenly and coated the cooking surface. Then she emptied the mud, feather, foot gunk, etc. into the left side of the skillet.

Spork didn't bother to tap my stolen egg against a hard surface and then split the eggshell in half. She wound up like a major league baseball pitcher, nicknamed Three Strikes, and dunked the egg into the skillet like basketball legend, Fly Nice. The shell instantly Humpty Dumpty'd and leaked out egg white and yolk guts. Surprisingly enough, she was able to keep the egg on the right of the skillet and the shark knuckle ingredients on the left by using her shoe liner as a divider. Oh, my poor egg!

When the egg cooked enough to create a sturdy foundation for the shark knuckles, Spork used a metal spoon to heap the shark knuckle creation onto the egg platform. Then, she used a fly swatter (her version of a spatula) to fold the uncovered egg on top of Mount Shark Knuckle. It actually looked just like an omelet that anybody could get from a restaurant. Spork tried to use the fly swatter to lift the omelet out of the cast iron skillet and place it on a dirty plate, but the omelet was too heavy. Finally, she grabbed a small broom and dustpan from under her hat and managed to maneuver the egg creation from point A to point B. In no time, she had the omelet on the plate.

I guess the funk-a-rific smell of Spork's valued meal had no effect on anybody in the class. Mr. Quiet was still playing his handheld video game that funneled loud music to his head phones and into his ears. I'm sure he'll be deaf by next year, if he keeps that up. Lenny was hiding behind his newspaper and calling Mr. Quiet a "Big-Headed Hobbit." He'll be here until Mr. Quiet goes deaf. For Lenny's sake, let's just hope Mr. Quiet doesn't learn how to read lips. Urhiness was still gawking and gazing in the mirror, as usual. She'll be in fifth grade for a long time. Me, I was still in Yummy Gummy Worm and lemonade-land. Snooze was, well, you know, still snoozing.

CHAPTER 10

The Serving

I was removed from my meditation by the sound of the dinging triangle (the music class one) that Spork used to let Mr. Quiet know his next meal was ready. Mr. Quiet pushed "pause" on his game and took off his headphones.

Mr. Quiet said, "This better be good, or you'll fail again."

"The Pork is chopped and foiled again!" said Lenny, before giving a sly, wooden grin.

Mr. Quiet calmly replied, "If she fails, she will do so right along with you, Lenny. Your negative attitude will give me the pleasure of seeing you tomorrow. Plus, my head size is in the 50th percentile and I'm too tall to be a Hobbit."

Mr. Quiet broke out some fine utensils for his meal. The platinum set included a fork, knife, and spoon with diamond encrusted handles. The silverware must have cost Mr. Quiet a fortune. He placed a silk napkin on his lap and tucked another into the collar of his red shirt. He was extra careful not to put his elbows on the table. After all, most ten-year-olds have learned their manners. This is probably an area where he can teach me a few tricks.

Spork started walking the steamy "food" toward Mr. Quiet and said, "Mr. Quiet, I present to you, a Shark Knuckle Omelet."

Mr. Quiet said, "Stop right there, Spork. I want Wrinkles to be our delivery boy. Rumor has it, Wrinkles delivers pizza for some local dollar store for a living."

At that point I was shocked because I couldn't figure out how he knew what I do for a living. I don't remember ever delivering pizzas to the Quiet household. Wow, Mr. Quiet sure does his homework. As I pushed those thoughts aside, I realized I felt nervous because, if I fell down like I normally did, then Spork would probably fail. Spork detoured to my desk, put the plate down in front of me, mumbled, "Thanks," and walked away. The heat-activated foot stench of a meal smelled horrendous.

To my surprise, I noticed the sticker on top of the omelet. Right away, it reminded me of two things. My first thought was the sticker was the symbol of a cherry on top of the perfect dessert. I smiled. Spork might actually pass the class. I felt so happy for her that I could have accidentally crushed my egg with my excitement. I squeezed my hand and the round object sprung back into shape. I completed my second thought when I realized I wasn't feeling gooey egg guts in my hand. One glance let me know there was a squeezable globe in my hand. The lip lifting grimace on my face told everyone in the room that I, Wrinkles Wallace, had been bamboozled and led astray. Spork took advantage of me! She stole my egg while I drifted off, and used it for this Shark Knuckle Omelet.

I covered up the globe, slid it inside my jacket pocket, walked up to Mr. Quiet, and placed the plate of nasty in front of him. He looked hungry.

"Thanks, Garçon," said Mr. Quiet. I took this as an insult because Garçon is French for "waiter." I'm a delivery man, not a waiter. I turned, walked toward my desk, and gave Spork the Dork (I'll pass that one to Lenny) an evil eyeball full of dirty look. She was looking at the ceiling and had five pairs of good luck fingers crossed. The only reason I was able to keep my composure was because I heard Grandma Wilbur's voice in my head saying, "Wrinkles, be cool." Grandma Wilbur was right, so I relaxed and thought about the good news that had just developed. See, the good news was, with the way Spork cooks, I knew I'd have plenty of time to teach her a lesson about stealing. Revenge, a dish best served with something Spork cooks, would be mine at all costs. That was, of course, as long as Mr. Quiet didn't enjoy the Shark Knuckle Omelet.

CHAPTER 11

The Meal

When I sat back down, Mr. Quiet was cutting a portion of the omelet. He lifted it up to his mouth to take a bite. Urhiness turned her back to him so she could see him through her mirror. Lenny shook his head. I rolled my eyes. Spork looked at me and then crossed her eyes for some extra luck. Snooze mumbled "Eggs 'n Lint" or "excellent." Either way, it made sense. The fork imported a piece of Shark Knuckle Omelet into Mr. Quiet's mouth and exported emptiness. That bite would be known as, "The Bite Heard 'Round the Classroom." I'm sure it would be in the history books of Old Endings Preparatory, if we ever wrote one.

Mr. Quiet paused after the first bite. He gave a blank look to everyone in the class. He definitely had his poker face on. Based on his facial expression, we had no clue if he liked the omelet or not. I mean, I know I would have catapulted that mess out of my mouth, but Mr. Quiet was calm about it.

We all figured he liked the meal when he started devouring it, one platinum fork-full after another. Mr. Quiet's lower jaw started moving like an elevator gone haywire. His mouth kept going up, down, and shimmying from left to right. I could hear the eggshells crack and crumble from meeting their fate with his molars. And then the omelet was gone. Mr. Quiet dropped his utensils with a loud clunk and the knife fell on the floor. His table manners were declining by the minute.

Spork was ecstatic. I guess Mr. Quiet usually spits the entire first bite out and dumps the rest of the meal into his trash. This time, he didn't. Spork began packing up her belongings and started heading for the door, ready to fill out an application to be a chef somewhere nearby. There are three restaurants within walking distance of the school. I guess she wants to stay close, so she can still make us her "nourishing meals."

Me, I was upset, seething, and beside myself. I had wasted an egg before even leaving the classroom. How would I ever pass fifth grade if I kept losing eggs in the classroom? Looking on the bright side, I wouldn't have to look out for a thief-a-holic's hands, sure to continue trying to steal my egg.

CHAPTER 12

The Dessert

All of a sudden, Mr. Quiet winced. His stomach grumbled like a lion with a toothache. It sounded like an epic battle during World War III. Mr. Quiet used his tongue to collectively shove any leftover food from his gums to the back of his throat. He sucked his teeth, pulled out a dental pick and let out a burp that would scare a full-grown Tyrannosaurus. We all saw the plague coming out of his mouth, like a storm of bumble bees were released, and the stench was the stingers. I imagined the Shark Knuckle Omelet with the nacho cheese chips from earlier engaging in a wrestling ribcage match. Mr. Quiet was sweating, and honestly, he didn't look so good.

Mr. Quiet announced, "Spork, that omelet was delectable. I like how you substituted hard-to-find ingredients, like shark knuckles, with tofu and other items. That was truly remarkable. The toe-like ingredient was amazing! It was a little tough, but as any good chef knows, toes are hard to identify. Now, I know you improvised and created your own toe-food that most would not dare to eat."

Mr. Quiet looked like Grandma Wilbur after a plate full of raw onions and hot peppers. His eyeballs were starting to roll, but he still spoke rather eloquently, if I do say so myself. Mr. Quiet continued, "Well, I'm not most people. I began biting my toenails at age three. I'm no stranger to this delicacy. I admit, yes, I do still munch on my toenails from time to time. I even figured out the best temperature to soak them in when I want to get tender and chewy toenails. One thing I *know* is how to properly prepare toenails. I think the way you utilized two species of toenail represents the essential variety needed to make this meal a pleasant surprise."

By now Spork was packed and ready to go. She'd already waved her goodbyes to everyone except me, and was almost free, when Mr. Quiet finished his speech.

He concluded, "Anybody who knows me knows that I do like pleasant surprises. However, what many fail to realize is, a pizza is not pizza without pizza sauce. Pizza without sauce is merely despicable cheese bread. As a professional watcher of the Hungry Channel and your teacher, I have to know the difference. Furthermore, an omelet is not an omelet without eggs. Your eggs were perfectly scrambled. They surrounded the omelet ingredients like a moat around a castle. And like any moat, there must be a dragon to protect the occupants of the castle. Potential castle party crashers are afraid of dragons, not dragon bones. Sporky, frankly, I'm afraid of your egg shells, not your eggs. The shells in the omelet were unacceptable. You know what that means, right?"

Spork nodded.

"You fail," said Mr. Quiet and struck his desk with a gavel that came out of nowhere.

Nobody knew anything about any dragons and eggs or whatever Mr. Quiet was talking about, but we understood that Spork (that egg-swindling slickster) was staying in the class. I smiled because Spork deserved to fail for stealing my egg.

As Spork started plugging in her equipment, my parade was drenched. Mr. Quiet said, "And you are a failure too, Wrinkles."

Instantly, my hand smacked down on my desk and created a frustrating thud that got Snooze's attention.

Snooze gave his best Dr. Martin Luther King, Jr. impression and said, "Let there be nonviolence in the face of violence. Let freedom ring from the mighty upstairs of Old Endings Preparatory..."

The rest was lost in the sound of snore.

CHAPTER 13

The Thoughts

I sat there and thought things through. Mr. Quiet wasn't going to do anymore teaching today, so all that was left to do was sit around and listen to Snooze snore, ignore Lenny when he opened his big mouth, breathe in the toxic waste from Spork's kitchen, try to make eye contact with Urhiness while she looked in her mirror all day long, and wait for Mr. Quiet to fail us. Basically, we were a bunch of failures waiting to fail yet again.

That's when something Grandma Wilbur once told me jumped to the front of the line in my brain. She always told me that in order for things to change, people have to start working together. *We* would have to somehow start working together. While at first I didn't think it would do us much good, I quickly realized that working together was better than sitting in class all day, waiting to fail. I mean, what did we have to lose? On one hand, it might not work, but on the other…

I took a look around the class to really see who we were. We were different, from our age to our appearance, but we did have some things in common. We were all students and we wanted out of Mr. Quiet's fortress of a classroom. Somehow we needed to figure out how to become a five-person team that did not act like a group of bumbling knuckleheads. At that point, in my mind, it was us against him. It was almost like a war and we were going to have to outthink, outsmart, and overpower this 10-year-old, if it was the last thing we did.

The echoing thoughts of Mr. Quiet calling me a "failure" led to step one of "Operation Team." If we could present a unified front (work together), we could beat Mr. Quiet at his own game; we just had to think about how to use Sittin' B. against himself. We had the age advantage, and hopefully, we were smarter. Hopefully. We had to find his weaknesses, figure out our strengths in the same area, and do what was needed to win.

CHAPTER 14

The Quitters

Before even knowing what came out of my mouth, I screamed, "I quit!" Maybe this is what Grandma Wilbur meant when she used to say, "I have to back out of the parking spot to leave the lot."

"I'm a quitter, he's a quitter, wouldn't you like to be a quitter, too?" replied Lenny in his fingers-down-the-chalkboard way of talking.

To our surprise, his voice cracked Urhiness' mirror in half and one piece fell to the floor. She didn't even bother to pick up the broken half. I guess seeing half of herself was better than seeing nothing, and at least she could still focus on her good side. In my mind, Urhiness was halfway to graduating fifth grade. I thought, if we could somehow get the other piece to fall out, then she'd be passing fifth grade really soon.

Wow, was I wrong. The second her mirror crashed, Urhiness instantly believed she was at the back end of the seven-years-of-bad-luck line. She thought that breaking the mirror was going to be the reason she would be in Mr. Quiet's class for at least seven more years. In what sounded like the perfect growl, Urhiness said, "I quit!"

Spork, still distraught about the eggshells, decided to throw in her dirty kitchen towel and let the dirty dishwater drain out of the sink. She screamed, "I'm putting y'all on a hunger strike!"

Mr. Quiet looked at us and grinned. He said, "You towel-throwing, reset-button-hitting do-littles are not good enough to be here. It seems like you want to be failures for the rest of your miserable lives. Instead of working together to figure out a way to pass, you'd rather just quit. You're choosing to fail during the day. You'd probably fail at night, too. You can't count enough sheep to go to sleep. You're that baaaaaaad."

"Want to make a bet?" I replied with a sly grin. He had just repeated what the voice of Grandma Wilbur said in my head. If everything went right, we were going to pass soon. All I had to do was figure out how to get us students to work together.

"Sure do. I bet you will fail going to night school. Failures fail and quitters quit."

"Maybe we need to make him eat those words," said Lenny.

I said, "As if Spork cooked them herself." Spork rolled her eyes at me and shook a dirty wooden spoon in my direction. She thought it was my fault she had failed.

"Well then, there we have it. You all are going to Knight School," said Mr. Quiet.

"You mean, we are going to have to become knights?" asked Urhiness.

"Sure do," replied Mr. Quiet with disgust in his eyes. Either he had deep resentment for us, or he needed to get to a bathroom as soon as possible. Mr. Quiet continued, "You're going to be the Knights of Night School."

Snooze said, "Knighty night, everybody."

CHAPTER 15

The Plan

I hadn't planned for us to become knights, but I'd do anything to pass. Besides, I knew that us going to night school would be an issue for Mr. Quiet. Now, if I could only pull off the nearly impossible and convince my classmates. The perfect opportunity came to me when Mr. Quiet's stomach started talking with an imaginary megaphone. Mr. Quiet's lips tightened and he looked up and to the left. He grabbed his stomach, a comic book, and darted off to the bathroom in the front corner of the classroom. The Shark Knuckle Omelet was on the move.

While Mr. Quiet was in his *office*, I only had a few minutes to gather my classmates and make sure we were on the same page. I whispered, "We can beat him at his own game."

"Shut up, Tinkles!" yelled Lenny. I could tell he was trying to get me in trouble with Mr. Quiet for talking.

I whispered, "I'm serious, folks. All we have to do —"

"I said, 'Shut up', Twinkles!" interrupted Lenny. I could tell he was mad about having to miss out on yelling at the contestants on his favorite evening game show for answering the questions wrong.

I replied, "Well, Lenny, you don't have to be involved, but the rest of us are getting out of here."

"How?" whispered Spork. "Don't you know that cooking at night can be dangerous? What if I fall asleep at the oven?"

"Food makes me sleepy," murmured Snooze.

"That's the plan," I said. "We are all used to staying up late. Teachers Mr. Quiet's age all go to sleep around one o'clock in the morning at the latest. If he's asleep we cannot fail because he won't know what we are doing. So, while Mr. Quiet's snoring, the classroom won't be boring."

"I'll tell him!" yelled Lenny. "I'll tell him everything!"

"Lenny," said Urhiness in a calming voice. "Come on, help us out."

"I'll let you talk about my cooking every night until we pass," said Spork. "And maybe you guys could give me some tips on what to cook so I can pass."

I added, "And Lenny, I'll let you talk about Snooze as much as you want while he and Mr. Quiet are asleep. We know you can't just stop talking about people overnight."

Snooze snored out what we all accepted as his approval.

"I guess so," mouthed Lenny. "But if I don't get my chance to say exactly what's on my mind to Sleeping Ugly over there, the deal is off."

"Lenny, you have to stop that," whispered Urhiness.

Spork pointed toward Urhiness' mirror and said, "You have to stop that, too." Urhiness closed her eyes and a tear dropped down her cheek.

"I know. It's just so hard to stop looking," replied Urhiness. Spork walked over and gave her a big hug.

Snooze let out a snore that sounded like he was trying to say, "Aww."

I gave a quick look around the room and declared, "All in favor say, 'Knights of the Night'."

"Knights of the Night," everyone replied in eerie harmony. This meant the stork had delivered our newly born, "Operation Team." We had plenty of work to do, but if we worked together, we could do it.

CHAPTER 16

The Crusade

When Mr. Quiet erupted out of the portable bathroom, I kept watching him. In fact, I couldn't take my eyes off him. I was getting to know his mannerisms fairly well. He would continuously change his facial expressions to mess with us. One minute he would be upset. Then he'd look like he was about to cry. He would give a grin that the untrained eye might consider a half-smile. With all of his facial trickery, I knew his twisted mind was up to something sinister. I had to figure out how to solve this puzzle, or we were doomed.

As much as I was learning about Mr. Quiet, I knew Mr. Quiet was learning about us as well. He had to know I was up to something. Like so many other teachers, he could sense a student luring him into a trap. He had to know we were going to try and team up to beat him and pass the class.

Being as smart as he is, Mr. Quiet also knew that I didn't know the first thing about being a knight. I did know the fancy metal armor and weapons they wore when they were riding horses. I did know how uncomfortable it looked for them to be walking around in suits made of hunks of metal. I also knew that on hot days, that metal could really heat up. I also remembered learning about how the sun reflecting off the metal might blind someone.

Then there was the thought of Mr. Quiet making us wear our knight clothes and making us ride that quarter horse downstairs. That thing could injure Lenny before it even warmed up. I bet Spork would be trying to kick the side of it to tenderize the meat for soup. Snooze would be asleep behind the saddle. Of course, Urhiness' hair would get messed up, and I'd crack my egg quicker than you could imagine. We were doomed if he made us ride that horse. I didn't even want to think about what would happen if he released the lion on us.

My own thoughts were interrupted when Mr. Quiet announced, "All you need to learn about chivalry will come from me. You need to understand that everything you already know about chivalry is dead. I don't open doors for others. I slam doors in their faces. I don't work with other people toward a common goal. I remain selfish. The world belongs to me. I own it. I am the most important person in that world that belongs to me. If things don't go my way I lie, cry, whine, pout, moan, groan, roll my eyes, whisper under my breath, and if all else fails, stick my bottom lip out and cross my arms."

Mr. Quiet paused to take a deep breath and I asked, "Are you sure?"

Mr. Quiet snapped back, "Wrinkles, nobody interrupts my speech! Now where was I?"

Snooze snored out, "Good Knightzzzzzzzz."

Mr. Quiet said, "It's good to see someone has been listening." He gave the rest of us a disgusted look and continued, "Oh yeah, good knights. As a group of good knights, you all are supposed to protect the King and the world that he rules. Well, I'm that King, and you five foolish failures will protect me at all times. I don't want to get hurt, so you will instead. I'm tired of lying, crying, whining, pouting, moaning, groaning, rolling my eyes, whispering under my breath, and sticking out my bottom lip and crossing my arms. From now on, you five will handle all of that."

At once, I realized that Mr. Quiet truly did not want us to succeed. His little motivational speech only showed me that he wanted to embarrass us older folks and make it look like he was the sane one. Knights are noble and I always thought chivalry was a good thing. Mr. Quiet wanted us to be foolish jesters who would take the blame for his pathetic and spoiled, bratty behavior. Can you imagine a world where adults whine and kids behave like they have some sense? Yeah, total craziness.

I kept Mr. Quiet's thoughts in the front of my head as I prepared for war because we needed to win in the worst way. Mr. Quiet continued, "We are going on a field trip. We are going across the street to Laura's for lunch. All of you knights are going to be my protection. You will all display chivalry through my eyes. You must behave like a group of ten-year-olds. Everyone must go and participate."

Suddenly, Mr. Quiet banged his gavel twice. A six foot wide hole appeared in the floor of our classroom. And wouldn't you know, out of the blue, a fireman's pole came down from our ceiling and traveled through the newly created hole in the floor. Before he could say, "case dismissed," Mr. Quiet was sliding down the fireman's pole to the first floor and was on his way to Laura's.

CHAPTER 17

The Motivating

I didn't think going to Laura's and acting like a bunch of ten-year-olds would be that big of a deal. I thought we would go in there, whine about anything and everything we could think of, and that would be it. Then we would leave while everyone thought we had never been in public before. No big deal, right?

WRONG!

I quickly realized that the hardest part of what Mr. Quiet said was that everyone must participate. How would we get Lenny across the street? How would we go about getting Snooze over there? Could we get Urhiness' eyes off her mirror long enough to even cross a street? Might Spork go over there, try to start cooking, and burn the building down? We needed teamwork and we needed it faster than I thought.

I looked at my classmates and said, "Gather around Lenny's chair and we'll figure out the best way to go to Laura's." Everyone gathered around except Snooze, who was still asleep. Urhiness, Spork, Lenny, and I tried to come up with a plan to at least get us all over to the restaurant.

It was apparent from the beginning that Lenny didn't want to have anything to do with walking over there. He said, "We aren't going to gain any real chivalry by going there in the first place. Mr. Quiet is sending us over there to make us look bad, while making him look good. If he makes me look bad, I'll make him look bad."

Lenny was probably right about us looking bad, but we had to at least give it a shot in order for the Knights of Night School thing to happen. Spork chimed in with something about how she hated restaurant food and doesn't eat just anybody's cooking, Urhiness was still half into her mirror, and, well, you know, Snooze snoozed.

It took about five seconds before I figured out what to say to convince them to go. "Urhiness, if we sit by the window, you'll be able to see yourself. That can help if you are having some trouble with your lack of mirror time. New rule, you can only look at your reflection for three seconds." She smiled and put her coat on. She slid down the fireman's pole as fast as Mr. Quiet did.

I rubbed my stomach and looked at Spork. I said, "Spork, you can look at the menu and see if there is anything on there that you can't cook. You can also find something that would be good for you to cook to pass the class." She smiled, grabbed her cookbook, and put her coat on. She slid down the fireman's pole as fast as Mr. Quiet did.

I turned my head and smiled at Lenny. I said, "Lenny, I know when you were younger, people rode around on chariots with horses pulling them. Well, unfortunately, we don't have a horse or a chariot. We do have my back, though.

I'll let you ride on my back across the street."

Lenny asked, "Can I use my whip to make you go faster like I did when I was younger?"

I answered, "Would you like to get dropped in the middle of the busy street?"

"Don't threaten me, Tinkles. I'll use the whip if I need to," Lenny replied. He put on his sweater. He was ready to go.

I went over to Snooze and whispered in his ear. "There is a booth you could lie on across the street. I'm sure it's comfortable and cozy. I'll even give you my jacket as a pillow. It's a waterproof pillow, so you can drool all you want." Snooze slowly rose, helped me out of my jacket, and began to sleepwalk toward the fireman's pole. He must not have realized that he needed to use the pole to get down like everyone else did. He just fell and hit the ground on the first floor with a horrendous splat. If he wasn't already sleeping, the way he hit his head on the floor would have definitely knocked him out.

I quickly wheeled Lenny over to the pole, tripped, and down went Lenny. I think Lenny called me all types of names during his fall to the first floor, but I could barely hear him because I was too busy shouting: "My Bad!"

Lucky for Lenny, he fell on top of Snooze and used him as a cushion. I slid down the pole and helped Lenny up onto my back. He instantly hit me with a whip that came out of nowhere. I thought he was just joking about whipping me.

"Ouch!" I screamed. "If you do that again I'm dropping you off at the Kindergarten room. They eat old fogies like you alive."

Lenny nervously replied, "No thanks, Pinkles. They'll want to sit on my lap and grab my beard. They'll pinch me and make loud noises and expect me to tie their shoes. Then they'll want to sing songs and tell me I'm older than fossils. Wrinkles, I'm allergic to those little goblins!"

"Well, then act as if you know better, or you'll have an allergic reaction of epic proportions."

Lenny slid his whip back into its hiding spot and we continued to the door.

CHAPTER 18

The Crossing

The girls had no problem crossing the street. Urhiness told Spork to follow her and used her mirror to look both ways before they crossed. Lenny and I also made it across without any real incident. He nearly hit me with the whip for not going fast enough, but he reconsidered when he saw a mile long line of eighteen wheelers driving southbound and a mile long line of city busses heading northbound. I think he realized if I let him off there, he was sure to be a goner.

Four out of five students had made it across the street in one piece. Eighty percent! And then there was Snooze. He was lazily bringing up the rear of our small convoy like a sleepwalking zombie. I imagined the busses and the eighteen wheelers about to make a sleep sandwich out of him and Spork hurrying back to scoop up the road kill for leftovers...well, let's not go there.

Just thinking about the disaster that was about to happen triggered my brain to do something to bring Snooze out of his slumber. If he didn't make it, we would all fail and he'd permanently be put to sleep. I couldn't let that happen, so I signaled with my right hand moving up and down for the truckers to blow their horns. They honked their booming horns as they zoomed past.

Snooze's reaction to the horn blasts was to defend himself with a sleepy martial arts fighting position. Then he started to sing the words, "Stop, do not hit Snooze! That truck will leave a bruise!"

Snooze used his left hand as a stop sign for a large navy blue truck going southbound. Then Snooze proceeded to walk out to the middle of the street. The trucks behind the navy blue truck weren't paying attention and they started to crash into one another. The crashing, horn blasting, and squealing of tires still weren't enough to wake him.

When it was all finished the navy blue truck's front bumper hit Snooze's left leg and tripped him. As Snooze got comfortable on the concrete, Lenny and I both knew he was about to become a human speed bump because, while he was out of potential southbound truck danger, he was about to encounter some real northbound bus danger.

At that point, Lenny was being his usual, mean self. He pulled out a red handkerchief to act as if the bus was a bull and he was a matador. Lenny thought the whole situation was so funny, he started celebrating the loss of Snooze in a joking manner. The handkerchief actually covered my eyes from what was about to happen with Snooze and the bus.

The next thing I knew, I snapped. I grabbed the handkerchief out of Lenny's hand and began yelling at him about his behavior.

I roared, "You ancient geezer! I wish —"

Crack! Lenny had pulled out his whip in self-defense and

cracked it at about the same time a bus full of kindergarteners stopped in front of us, opening its door. The bus driver was a large man with a green sweater and maroon pants. His face included a graying moustache with a captain's hat on top of his head.

The bus driver said, "You cannot get on a bus like this with weapons like that, and you both have to pay full price in order to ride. I know the old piggy-back-and-ride for half price trick."

Lenny's body started shaking on my back. Wow, he really was scared of the kindergarteners. I asked Lenny, "Are you sure you don't want to get on? I'll pay for you to go wherever those kindergarteners are going."

"Mr. Bus Driver," said Lenny, "keep it moving!"

The driver gave us a glare, closed the doors, and smoked the tires as he peeled off. I couldn't look at Snooze, or even in his direction. I just knew he was somewhere floating on cloud nine by now.

Quickly, I turned and ran into Laura's while ignoring the fact that Lenny was whipping me and yelling, "Giddy Up! ¡Andéle, arriba! Chop! Chop!" As we entered the first set of doors to the restaurant, Lenny grabbed my neck like it was the reins for a horse and pulled backward. I instantly stopped. Good thing I didn't have on a shock collar.

"Wrinkles, I need some candy from the machines. I need some Sour Boppers or I'll die. All this running has me feeling tired and weak."

"Oh, so you can call me by name when you want something. By the way, I'm the one doing all the running and you're the one on my back."

"Come on, Wrinkles. I need a little pick me up."

"I'm the one doing the real picking up. Besides, the only thing you've been picking up is your nose."

Lenny replied, "I've got a few places to put the —" I shook myself like a raging bull and tried to get him off my back. He held on tight and said, "I'll be nice. I promise. I'll play along with whatever your little idea for outsmarting Mr. Quiet turns out to be. If it's really good, I'll even give you a little help."

I thought about it for a split second. I would need his help. Meeting him halfway was kind of important.

"Come on Wrinkles," said Lenny with a little pleading in his voice.

"Okay," I answered as I fished two dull quarters from my front pocket. I put the money in the machines and twisted the knobs. The contents from both containers spilled into my hands. "Here you go, Lenny."

"I'm starving back here!"

In my excitement, I flicked the candy over my shoulder a little too hard. I'm sure I could have put out an eye or two, or at least got them stuck in the ceiling tiles. To my surprise, I didn't hear the sound of the candy hitting the ceiling and bouncing off the floor, or a yelp from Lenny. I looked through the reflection of the second set of double doors and saw what I thought was Lenny's neck lengthen like a giraffe, his jaw unhinge like a snake, and every single Sour Bopper landing in his open mouth.

I hurried through the second set of doors (before Lenny could get all anaconda on me) and into the restaurant. The door I opened accidently hit the fresh-brewed pot of coffee a waitress was holding as she walked by. While the waitress managed to avoid the splash of hot coffee, Lenny's leg was not so lucky. The waitress went to help Lenny, but he hadn't even noticed that the hot coffee hit his leg. That was odd, but thoughts of what happened to Snooze quickly came back to my mind.

I dashed over to the U-shaped booth to tell the others that Snooze didn't make it. I yelled, "Snooze got run over by a bus!"

"It was the craziest thing ever!" yelled Lenny. "A truck tripped him and the bus squashed him! We didn't see the entire thing because Dinkles over here got all clammy and turned away when it was about to happen. The bus driver even burned rubber on him! Rest in peace, Snooze."

Spork asked, "Since he won't be eating with us, did you guys get any of the leftovers for, well you know, leftovers?"

"No! Absolutely not!" I said. "How could you be thinking about food at a time like this?"

It was just then I looked down at the bench seat and saw the dirty bottom portion of Snooze's pajama feet hanging off the edge. He must have gotten up while we were talking to the bus driver.

"Snooze! How did you make across the street?" I asked.

Urhiness answered for him. She explained, "Everybody knows that cats have nine lives and Snooze has at least twelve snooze bars. That makes a dozin'. He uses them to help him cross the street. He probably used the snooze bar to give him a moment to get up and cross the street before the bus could hit him.

Snooze let out an ear bone bending snore, which meant he agreed, and all was well again. I put Lenny in an adult-sized booster seat, sat my back pockets on the plastic next to Mr. Quiet, and took a good look around the restaurant.

CHAPTER 19

The Field

Laura's was a fairly nice establishment. Based on what I had heard about the place, the food was better than decent and the prices were affordable. From what I could tell, the owner was a retired major league baseball pitcher with a serious fastball.

Around the restaurant, he had pictures of himself on the field. The western wall of Laura's had a refrigerated dessert area that held a variety of pies, rice pudding, carrot cake, and an assortment of salad dressings. The cash register was a typical tan color and let out the words "HOME RUN!" every time it was opened. The counter area had five wooden stools that swiveled clock-wise and counter clock-wise to allow customers to spin while parking their pants on those seats.

The rest of the restaurant consisted of a few booths that looked like the one we were sitting in. There were also rectangular tables, each with two to four mismatched chairs. On the tables were syrup, sugar, Not-so-Sweet, jam, jelly, salt, pepper, hot sauce, ketchup, mustard, a napkin dispenser, and laminated menus with bent corners. The front of the tri-fold menu had pictures of perfectly prepared meals with fries that looked crispy and delicious, and sharing the same plate was a cheeseburger created by a food artist. One thing was for sure, Spork didn't make any of the pictured meals.

Just by looking around the restaurant let me know that the bulk of Laura's lunch crowd came from the nearby automotive plant that had an hour-long lunch break, students at Old Endings Preparatory, and retirees. The students would sneak over to Laura's during their lunchtime to avoid the school lunch. Rumor around school was that Spork catered the lunches at Old Endings and nobody wanted to eat the food. Once the students realized Spork was inside the restaurant, they instantly lost their appetite and started to leave. It was clear that anyone who recognized Spork wanted no part of any food she managed to get near. People took out restraining orders on Spork to keep her at least one hundred feet from their food.

After taking in the scene, I began looking at my menu. My mouth was watering for a crumbled Caramel Toffee Crisp candy bar on pita with extra mayonnaise and crushed hot corn flakes. That was when Mr. Quiet started sharing his thoughts on knights and chivalry.

Mr. Quiet said, "I'll admit, I didn't think you all would make it over here. Now that you are here, we have to get this chivalry stuff off the ground. In order to protect the King, you all need to be ready to fight in my honor —"

Lenny interrupted, "I didn't come over here to fight."

"Me neither," said the rest of us.

"I'm not talking about punching and kicking. Maybe a little game of catch," said Mr. Quiet.

For some reason, playing a game of catch in the restaurant of a former major league baseball pitcher didn't sound like a great idea to me.

Mr. Quiet continued, "The first step is to order complicated meals and complain about what you get when you receive them."

"What about cost?" asked Urhiness. "I don't have any spare money for food!"

"Don't worry about cost," he replied.

I smiled. Mr. Quiet was going to treat us to some good eating. He was actually going to crack open his piggy bank and buy us lunch. I had to make room in my stomach for a creation that would surely disable a weaker man.

I quickly came to my senses when Lenny said, "Urhiness, it's no big deal. I'm sure Stinkles will take care of the bill." He winked at me and smiled with those tree bark teeth. He slicked me again.

"My thoughts exactly," replied Mr. Quiet.

How could I help us win this war when it seemed like Lenny was working for Mr. Quiet? I thought Lenny and I had come to an understanding about him helping me. That runt! If he knew I didn't want to pay for his Sour Boppers, he certainly knew I didn't want to pay for lunch. Nevertheless, I quickly realized that I had gotten us into this mess and was determined to get us out of it.

Finally, I said, "Yeah, okay, I'll put it on my credit card."

"Just as I knew you would," said Mr. Quiet. "Now that we have that settled, there are a few other things you need to know. The staff here is our enemy. We must conquer them like old General Hannibal did in Northern Italy. Besides, like Hannibal, one of us arrived on an elephant."

Lenny smiled and I guessed that I was the elephant.

Urhiness said, "Hey, they look like friendly people to me."

Mr. Quiet continued, "Oh well. We're not here to make friends. We are here to be an influence on others. We are going to take them by surprise. When they try to get revenge, we will no longer be at school because they close at 4:00 p.m. That means they won't be able to get back at us. I am Commander Quiet and you all are my army."

Some army we were. Our commander was getting crazier by the minute. It was bad enough that we were over at Laura's, but now he was using us as his own personal army of knights.

Maybe we were all too focused on Mr. Quiet's plans because none of us noticed a fishing line tied to a chair sitting across from us. As a waiter walked by, Mr. Quiet yanked the line, causing him to trip. While the waiter managed to stay on his feet, he did spill lunch for three people all over the floor. There were French fries flying, onion rings rolling, and chicken tenders tumbling everywhere. Mr. Quiet had truly caught the waiter (and us) by surprise.

"Spork, you better —" Mr. Quiet said.

"You're reading my mind. That's practice food for recipe research." She grabbed the broom and dustpan from under her hat and began to make it look like she was being helpful. The other employees were too busy laughing and calling the waiter a klutz to notice that this was the first official casualty of what will forever be known at Old Endings Preparatory as: "The Battle at Laura's."

Meanwhile, Spork swept the pile over to our booth and stuffed all the food into a bag she had waiting. She was extra excited to actually get some good ingredients. I bet she was probably thinking of the perfect way to reorganize the meals that fell on the floor and claim them as her own. Too bad Mr. Quiet knew the food had been on the floor and would probably refuse to eat it. Probably. Although, the thought of Mr. Quiet eating the Shark Knuckle Omelet made me think twice.

CHAPTER 20

The Pitch

Our waitress came over and stood in front of us. She looked about twenty-five years old. Her hair was in a ponytail that traveled to the shoulders of her red t-shirt. Her black apron clung to her sides and was overflowing with napkins and straws. Her black pants hung over the back of her dirty white tennis shoes because they were a little too long. She had two earrings in each ear, one in her nose, and hanging from the necklace on her neck was a small gold charm that read #1 Mom. She kept making those impatient popping noises with her gum as she waited to get our attention. It was obvious she didn't want to be at the restaurant.

She finally broke the silence with, "Let me guess, you cheapskates want water with extra lemons and sugar, for starters."

"How'd you know?" I asked.

"I know free lemonade makers when I see them. I can spot 'em from 5,280 feet away." She placed her left hand on her hip and rolled her eyes.

"Ma'am," said Mr. Quiet.

"The name tag says Sharon, if you can read."

"Sharon, we'll have real lemonade," said Mr. Quiet, with a spoonful of charm that was much better than what he did for the waiter he had just tripped a moment ago. He continued, "And by the time you get back with it, we'll be ready to order. We're as hungry as twenty-two termites sharing a toothpick."

"Yeah, whatever you say, Sonny." Sharon turned and walked away with an attitude.

I called out, "Can I get mine without ice?" but got no reply. If Sharon did hear me, she sure did know how to play it off like she didn't.

Mr. Quiet, on the other hand, wasn't in the ignoring mood. "She called me 'Sonny.' Of course, you all know this means war. Anybody want to pass the chivalry test? Well then, do as I say, and start right now."

"Okay," we said together.

It took about a minute for Sharon to come back with all of our drinks. Everyone else had glasses that were practically filled to the rim with ice and there couldn't have been much more than a squirt of lemonade in each glass. That's the reason why I usually don't get ice in my drinks. On the other hand, my glass of lemonade was steaming. It must have been made with the same water they use for their extra hot tea, because I could see the top of the plastic glass starting to melt from the heat. Who knew they used all that ice to cool down the lemonade?

"What do you want now?" was the question Sharon asked to let us know she was ready to take our orders. She clutched her notebook and began scrolling without looking up. Her facial expressions were blank the entire time we ordered, and, I mean, there were some things I couldn't imagine ever eating.

Urhiness ordered a kiddy-sized, stir-fried waffle and a bologna hoagie with extra onions and ice cream on it. She stopped after looking in the mirror because she didn't want to gain any weight. Lenny decided on a brownie smothered in gravy and an omelet with cottage cheese and corned beef hash. Mr. Quiet chose a hamburger on a cinnamon roll with applesauce and hot peppers. I guess he wasn't really that hungry due to the Shark Knuckle Omelet that Spork made him earlier. Spork had chicken with cranberry sauce, served over rice pudding and mixed vegetables. She also ordered a grilled gizzard-and cheese-and-macaroni sandwich. Snooze said nothing. He managed to put his hand on the table. His order was scribbled on his hand. Sharon copied down his request for a bowl that basically was hash browns and turkey (the tryptophan in it could be used as a sleeping aid), all swimming in decaffeinated coffee. For dessert, he wanted to wash it down with a root beer float with mashed potatoes instead of ice cream.

I was feeling quite hungry and creative. I ordered pancakes topped with chili, whipped cream, fried oysters, and sauerkraut. I had a taste for a peanut butter and jelly pork chop sandwich. I also needed a slab of ribs dipped in mayonnaise with extra black pepper and I craved a tuna fish and syrup pita. For dessert I ordered apple pie and mushrooms with blue cheese dressing. Since my lava lemonade was hot enough to melt a glacier, I figured I'd have to order something else. The perfect drink to wash it all down was sweet and sour pickle juice. I just relish those. I even asked to have the glass come with a sliced piece of sausage that would be a lemon. The *cherry* of the drink would be a rarely eaten third portion of a chicken wing. Not the drumstick or that two-boned piece, but the other funny looking piece.

Sharon whirled away without even checking to make sure she had everything right. Talk about lousy service. I was sure she wouldn't be getting a tip. When she came back without the food and had a bill in-hand, I got worried.

Sharon barked, "You guys might decide to skip out on your bill. I need you to pay right now and in cash."

"No credit card?" I asked.

"Not when you can dispute the charge and stiff the restaurant out of money. You think this is our grand opening? We're not as dumb as you look."

How dare she insult my looks! Grandma Wilbur always said I was as handsome as a hog in hot water. Instead of telling Sharon what Grandma Wilbur thinks, I asked everyone to turn their heads and I fished inside my left sock for the cash. The meals came to a total of just under $100 and I happened to have one hundred dollars in ones. This was my lucky day.

I handed Sharon the money and said, "Keep the change."

"Thanks, Mr. Big Tipper. With the change from here and the dime on the floor under your booth, I might be able to get some Sour Boppers out of the machines over there."

"No problem, Sharon."

In a moment, our food arrived. Sharon's two arms were filled with our plates of food. She began calling out the orders and giving them to us with a smile. She was smiling. Maybe it was because she was actually trying to earn her tip. Maybe the smell of our food left her with no choice but to smile. When she finished passing out the orders, she turned and walked away without saying a word.

CHAPTER 21

The Hit

As bad as I wanted to dive into my food, I found out it didn't matter what food Sharon put in front of us because Mr. Quiet wasn't going to let us eat it anyway.

Mr. Quiet barked, "Don't touch the food! Do not put one fork to your greedy, big mouths. We are at war here. We aren't here to eat this mess that the enemy cooked for us. We are at war. Do you hear me?"

"Yes," we all grumbled with the excitement of dead bugs. From the look on everyone's faces, except Mr. Quiet's, I got the feeling that we really were ordering the food to at least see how it would taste. Too bad Mr. Quiet had other plans for what we would do with my one hundred Washingtons worth of food.

Mr. Quiet continued, "This food is to be used as ammunition for the war we are about to wage against this entire restaurant. We'll be doing the throwing and they'll be doing the catching."

"Aside from Sharon being a little rude, I'm not sure why we are at war," said Urhiness.

I added, "Plus, the other customers are here to eat, just like we are. I didn't pay all that money for the food to be used in a food fight."

Spork jumped in and said, "Yeah! We can't waste this good food!"

Mr. Quiet snapped, "Oh, stop it, you three. The customers are here to support the staff, just as you are here to support your King. When that rude waitress comes back, I'll do all of the talking. You all just sit here and look unhappy. Stick your lips out and pout. If you can manage to squeeze out a tear, then you'll make me feel really good."

"Why are we *really* waging war, Mr. Quiet?" asked Lenny.

Mr. Quiet answered, "For your information, when I was six years old, I wanted to have my birthday party here and they wouldn't let me. So now I must have my revenge. Now, if you want to show chivalry, you'll keep your mouths closed and do what I say."

I couldn't believe it. We were going to war over something that happened four years ago. I had to waste my one hundred wonderful Washingtons and some great food in order for Mr. Quiet to get revenge for not being able to have his birthday party here at Laura's. Here, of all places! I mean, I could understand if the place had miniature golf or video games. Nope. This place was a regular restaurant that would be the last place I'd think a six-year-old would want to have a birthday party.

As Sharon walked from behind the counter with a pitcher of icy lemonade for us, we all poked out our bottom lips and gave her some seriously sad stares. I could tell that Sharon was puzzled after she saw us and noticed that we had not touched our food.

"How is everything?" Sharon asked.

We didn't dare say a word. It was Mr. Quiet's time to talk and we were only there to support his crazy cause.

When we didn't respond, Sharon added, "I brought out a pitcher, so everyone can keep their lemonade cooled at their own leisure. Can I get you something else, like ketchup or steak sauce?

"Absolutely not!" yelled Mr. Quiet. "I am appalled at the state of these meals! You shorted and skimmed us out of valuable ingredients! And, now you're being lazy and making us pour our own icy lemonade! Keep it up and we're going to ask for that tip back!"

"Wait. What?" asked Sharon while she tried to contain her anger. It was obvious she took pride in taking the correct order, as well as the cooks' presentations and artistic interpretation of each meal. Plus, I bet she was only trying to help us by keeping the icy lemonade at the table. And, everybody knows not to mess with a server's tips.

Mr. Quiet started putting his hands in our food and showing Sharon what his fake issues were. At that point I knew I wasn't going to eat anything he touched.

Mr. Quiet explained, "That's not how you make a peanut butter and jelly pork chop sandwich! Everybody knows that there must be crunchy peanut butter to give the pork chop that crunchy taste. And, who uses grape jelly anymore? The seeds in strawberry jelly provide extra objects for the chewer to enjoy as a healthy, midnight snack."

Sharon asked, "Why didn't Sir Stinky-Sock-Savings-Stasher over there say anything when I took his order?"

Mr. Quiet replied, "Why didn't you ask? Who stashes white gravy in their rice pudding? It blends in and doesn't promote color contrast. We needed the brown gravy that came from the pork chop grease, and a little flour and water. Also, why didn't the grilled gizzard-and-cheese-and-macaroni sandwich come with fried chicken residing in tomato soup? Everybody knows that grilled gizzard-and-cheese goes great with tasty tomato soup. Just like everyone knows that macaroni and cheese always comes with fried chicken at other restaurants. What kind of numbskull do you have back there cooking?"

"Actually, the numbskull is the owner."

"Oh, really? Well owning a dump like this has not helped his cooking skills."

"Is there anything else that is wrong with your order?" asked Sharon.

"Yes, as a matter of fact, it is all cold now, so we won't be able to eat it. We want a refund!"

"I'm going to get the owner," said Sharon.

"Look Sharon," said Mr. Quiet. "It's my birthday and we came to celebrate. You go get the owner, and when you come back, bring the money for the food, and your tip, with you."

I wasn't sure if Mr. Quiet was actually a birthday boy, or if he was fibbing. If it was his birthday, I realized I could have pulled a few strings and got us some dollar pizzas delivered for a few John F. Kennedys.

I started to ask Mr. Quiet about his birthday when Sharon announced, "I'm sorry, Sonny, but we don't do birthdays around here. It's restaurant policy. We can put all of your stuff in the microwave to warm it up, but there will be no celebrating, no cake, no candles, no singing, no toasting lemonade, and no refunds." Sharon pointed to the sign *NO*

REFUNDS *or* EXCHANGES above the cash register and went to get the owner of the restaurant.

Mr. Quiet glared at her and said, "Go get him, Sharon-Baron-Bo-Baron...."

When Sharon walked around the counter and headed toward the cooking area, Mr. Quiet stuck his hand in my pickle juice, grabbed the piece of chicken wing, and hurled it at her. Sharon only felt the wind from the chicken wing, but that was enough to make her fall to the ground. Napkins and straws were everywhere. I couldn't believe he actually threw the piece of wing at her and managed to get it stuck into the wall! I could only imagine what would have happened if he actually hit her with it because the kid had a rocket for an arm.

"What are you doing? You don't throw pieces of chicken wings at people!" I yelled.

"Cool it," said Mr. Quiet. "I missed on purpose. I'm just warming up my arm for later."

Urhiness said, "But you could have hit her."

Mr. Quiet said, "Well, if it isn't Miss Mirror looking out for someone else for a change."

Urhiness shook her head at him.

"Mr. Quiet," said Lenny, "you better cool it before they call the police on you."

"Hush, Lenny. *You* want *me* to be the one who stops messing with people? Really? Aren't *you* the guy who always messes with people? It seems like you're the one starting to lose your edge. You're getting weak. You're changing. What happened to the Lenny that loved conflict?"

"I'm just saying," Lenny replied.

"I told you to hush. I have this situation under control," said Mr. Quiet.

Meanwhile, the rest of the customers had no clue as to what was going on. They were too busy stuffing their faces to even notice that the first pitch, although not a real STEEEERIKE, was clearly a *fowl* ball. Mr. Quiet acted like nothing happened. Sharon crawled under the double doors that led into the kitchen. I saw her eyes peek between the doors, then noticed her reach for the chicken wing piece that was stuck in the wall. I knew we were in for it, and I was probably going to be the one who was blamed. After all, how often was it that people ordered a little chicken wing in their drink?

I heard some loud noises coming from the kitchen. The owner was asking all types of questions about the food and why Sharon was crawling into the kitchen. A moment later, the owner came out of the kitchen, staring at our table.

The owner wore black and white checkered pants and a white button-up shirt. Over his shirt was a black, mid-thigh length apron with the words, *Kiss the cook, tip your waitress, and love thy owner* written in yellow. He had a pencil-thin mustache with hair handlebars and wore a hairnet over his completely bald head. His smile was phony bologna and we could tell. His hands were hiding behind his back and I saw the splatter of what looked like blood drop to the floor behind the owner. From the angle I was sitting at, I could see that he was hiding a large leather object behind his back. I could just make out that his left hand was inside a baseball mitt filled with meatballs drenched in tomato sauce. His right hand had a biscuit that he was gripping like a baseball.

Uh-oh.

CHAPTER 22

The Brawl

I yelled, "WATCH THE FASTBALL!" because of the owner's major league throwing arm. As I lowered my head to avoid getting hit by a biscuit, I saw Mr. Quiet fling the peanut butter and jelly pork chop sandwich at the owner. The pork chop went through the door to the kitchen and knocked some pots and pans to the ground. The owner ended up with a piece of jelly bread on his white shirt and a piece of peanut butter bread stuck to his cheek. Good thing for him, he didn't use crunchy peanut butter. Gravity helped drop the pieces of bread to the floor, right before the owner dabbed his biscuit into the jelly and then the peanut butter. He took a quick bite and let out a mighty yell.

The sound of that mighty yell was more than enough to catch the attention of the rest of the restaurant. The owner, who must have been in plenty of food fights before, ducked behind the counter. The customers followed his lead and hid underneath their tables. The other workers at the restaurant ran out the front doors. Perhaps they had just quit their jobs.

At that moment it felt like the World Series was traveling through the restaurant like a curveball. Quickly, the owner rose from behind the counter and pitched a zinger in our direction. He caught Snooze at the peak of a snore and fired the meatball straight into the middle of his mouth. Snooze chewed and swallowed, then mumbled, "Let the games begin."

Instantly, Sharon came out of the kitchen with an ice cream scoop and a pot of mashed potatoes. She was scooping and hurling them like snowballs. We were in the middle of a "Buffet Battle Royale" and we needed to start serving up some mini-sliders of our own.

Mr. Quiet growled and yelled, "FOOD FIGHT!"

He whizzed a cinnamon roll U.F.O. (Uneaten Food Object) at the owner that curved around the owner's big, bald head and managed to take his hairnet clean off. Wow, Mr. Quiet was really cutting it close when it came to missing on purpose!

For some reason, I thought us Knights were somehow going to avoid doing any real damage in the food fight. That is, until I saw Lenny grab some ketchup and mustard bottles and start spraying customers with their contents. One little boy in a tan coat ended up looking like a human hotdog. Then Lenny unscrewed the top of the pepper and flung the black dust in the direction of the competition. The customers began sneezing and none of them even bothered to cover their mouths.

Prior to Lenny attacking with chemical warfare, the customers had been neutral. Afterwards, they started throwing their food at us, too. Some liver and onions barely missed my head, when I had an idea. I leaned over and whispered into Snooze's ear, "Lie across the table and stretch out on your side. It will help your food digest." Snooze climbed up on the table while being pelted by mixed vegetables. Carrots, green peas, lima beans with bits of smoked turkey, broccoli, and cauliflower were practically planted in his clothing. Snooze's lying down provided the rest of us with a much-needed cover from the flying food, including the rib bones and chicken legs that hit the back of the booth and came to rest in the cushions. That's when I called a quick meeting. Everyone but Snooze joined me under the table.

"What do we do, King Quiet?" asked Spork.

"We have to show them who's boss and then leave before they go back into the kitchen for reinforcements. I saw a delivery truck being unloaded, so they have enough food to go into extra innings."

Spork replied, "Well, I have the food I swept up, the food we ordered, and they keep throwing more."

"Urhiness, use your mirror to see where the majority of the food that is hitting Snooze is coming from," said Mr. Quiet. She raised the mirror and managed to get a glimpse of the room before her mirror was hit by a mashed potato snowball that was topped with a spaghetti meatball. We instantly knew Sharon and Baldy were real competition.

All I could think was how to win the battle, but I also had to think about getting us out of there. Boom, I had another plan. I grabbed the syrup from the tabletop and brought it back down with a glob of potato on my knuckle. I unscrewed the top of the syrup and tossed its contents out of the glass container and onto the floor near Sharon and the owner. Spork grabbed the sugar packets and my hot lemonade. Then Spork rapidly poured the sugar packets into my hot lemonade. It began to look like lemony syrup.

"Mr. Quiet, I'm ready to pass. I've made a perfect drink," said Spork.

She handed the hot and sweetened lemonade to Mr. Quiet. He took a sip and the sugar rushed to his brain. That much sugar could have killed a diabetic person, but it only intensified Mr. Quiet's desire to wage war. Ten-year-olds and sugar are a dangerous combination. His eyes were wide and fiery and his jaw muscles clenched.

"Spork, you have passed the drink portion of your exam. Now all you have to do is pass the meal portion." Spork jumped up in excitement and quickly came right back down because Sharon and the owner pelted her with their meat and potato combination. She returned with a meatball stain on her smock and a chin full of mashed potatoes. Meanwhile, Lenny must have been reading my mind because he threw the rest of Spork's passing lemonade in the same area I had thrown the syrup. Now we had the sticky floor we would need.

I reached up again and grabbed a leftover straw and a napkin to make a white flag for surrendering. I whispered, "I'm going to wave this flag and make them think we quit. Then, when they see we want peace, we'll bombard them and get our King out of here and back to safety."

"Kind of like how you all tried to make *me* think that you had quit," said Mr. Quiet. "Keep up the good lying, Wrinkles."

Mr. Quiet's sarcastic words stung. Maybe I shouldn't have yelled out a lie, but I felt like I had to get us out of Laura's at all costs. Too bad the cost of getting out of Laura's was me lying, Lenny continuing being mean, Urhiness using her mirror, and Snooze still sleeping. Even though Spork had passed her drink portion of 5th grade, the rest of us hadn't made any real progress. Yeah, we were finally starting to work as a team, but our cause was lousy and a perfectly good restaurant was now a mess. And, I still had to get us out of there.

I lifted my right hand in the air and waved the makeshift flag. All of the sudden the action stopped. Sharon walked over to the owner and they slapped baseball mitt and ice cream scoop together in triumph. They actually believed my lie.

CHAPTER 23

The Run

"Alright, come out with your hands up, you losers," said the owner. I propped Snooze's hands up with some silverware while Urhiness used her mirror to see the whereabouts of the opposition. In the meantime, Mr. Quiet and I put all the food we could gather into Spork's cooking bag without making a sound. We silently scraped the plates for any extra dressing and crumbs. When the bag was full, Mr. Quiet tied it loosely and the two of us lifted it up onto the seat.

Next, we managed to get Lenny back into his adult booster chair. He raised his arms in the sky to show defeat. Spork and Urhiness followed his lead and sat on each side of him. Mr. Quiet and I sat on either side of the cooking bag. That's when we all noticed the mega meatball that was sitting on a large wooden spoon that looked like a catapult. There was also a cannon stuffed with mashed potatoes to the right. We were in trouble.

The owner stood with his head up high and his chest

puffed out. He yelled, "How dare you come into my restaurant and attempt to wage war with my food! My customers and I will not be defeated!"

The customers roared with approval. We all sank down in our seats, just a little bit.

The owner continued, "You had the audacity to order complex, complicated and creative meals, only to waste them. But, that's okay. I'll be adding those items to our new gourmet menu. Once people know you can get food like that here at Laura's, I'll be filthy rich."

Wow, unless I had spaghetti sauce in my ears, Spork might have a job waiting for her if she ever passed the rest of 5th grade. When she heard those words, she stood to let them know she was the person for the job. Sharon pulled the cord on the cannon and shot off a mashed potato missile that *just* missed Spork's head. While Sharon was mashing mashed potatoes against the wall, Mr. Quiet and I were positioning the contents of the bag to just the right place. The ingredients were starting to bubble, fizz, and smoke. Some sort of reaction was happening with that food.

Totally unaware of our brewing boulder, Sharon snarled, "SIT DOWN!" Spork did as she was told and Sharon continued, "I took your orders and brought all of your food quickly!" She paused and whined out, "What more do you want from me?"

Snooze, who had just inhaled to let out a snore as Sharon asked her last question, replied, "Dessert."

"He'll have apple pie surprise," said Mr. Quiet.

"We have apple pie, but no surprise. That is, unless the surprise is ice cream on top," said Sharon. Her natural waitress instincts kicked in full force, as she whipped out her pen and tablet to take down the order.

"Well, we'll hold the surprise then."

Mr. Quiet knew that we were, in fact, holding the surprise that was going to win us the series. The owner turned his back to get the apple pie from the dessert fridge while Sharon grabbed some silverware. Urhiness and Spork slid Lenny out of the booth and quickly dragged him out of the restaurant. The other customers were trying to let Sharon and the owner know, but they were so focused on getting the apple pie ready that they weren't listening.

With them distracted, Mr. Quiet and I (but mostly me) lifted the bag from its hiding spot. Mr. Quiet bit the top portion of the plastic bag like a grenade pin, spit it out (because we know that plastic can cover up your wind pipe and block your breathing), and we launched the bag toward the home team. I could hardly bear to look at the disaster we were sure to leave because we had just dropped a bomb of furious food. It was time to retreat.

I grabbed Snooze by his arm pits and used him as a human sleeping shield to protect Mr. Quiet from the tornado of trouble. Sharon and the owner had been blasted by rice pudding, gravy, pita surprise, and a bag full of other gunk. Mr. Quiet and I made it to the exit as the customers pelted Snooze with French fries and ice cubes.

Snooze responded, "Thank you. Please come again."

Just after the first set of doors closed behind us, the enormous meatball catapulted and cracked the glass. More missile mashed potatoes shot through the glass and hit the candy machines. That surely could have put all three of us in the hospital. The owner/waitress tag team gave chase until they stepped in syrup on the floor. That caused them to run out of their shoes and socks and they couldn't take another step. At once, their feet were stuck in defeat.

CHAPTER 24

The Victory

The three of us managed to make it across the street and back to the safety of Old Endings Preparatory before we could be blasted with their heavy artillery. We climbed our way into the classroom and rejoined our teammates to celebrate. Lenny was sitting in his chair like he had never left, Urhiness was in the mirror, and Mr. Quiet un-paused his game and continued to play. I put Snooze back in his chair. Meanwhile, Spork turned on the oven, then started toward Snooze. She used her fly swatter to scrape food off of him and flung it in a mixing bowl. She had a new idea for cupcakes or scones.

I was ecstatic. I knew in my heart that we had Mr. Quiet on the ropes and we were about to win another battle. He couldn't deny we had shown "chivalry" at Laura's.

Knights of Night School: 1

Mr. Quiet: 0

Let the night school battle begin!

The bell rang and it was time for our day to end. Mr. Quiet stood and made his final announcements.

"Well," he said, "This was a boring, first day. I'd expect this type of behavior from kindergarteners. But this certainly won't be tolerated in the future. It's time to leave. I have some cartoons to watch while my dad makes my fish sticks. But, I'll be seeing you Knights tonight."

"You mean, tomorrow," I said. "As in, we need to be back tomorrow night."

"Wrinkles, are you serious, or do you have a meatball for a brain? Of course I mean tonight! You all wanted this night school stuff and now you have it."

"Mr. Quiet, I'm serious. I thought we would have a night off. I have a dodgeball game tonight and I don't want to miss it."

Mr. Quiet responded, "So you're going to the dodgeball game, too? My mom makes a schedule every week and puts it on the refrigerator. According to my schedule, I have a dodgeball game tonight as well, so I guess I'll see you there. Please, don't forget to bring this precious egg with you, either. Consider it homework."

Lenny laughed at me.

Mr. Quiet said, "Just for that, the rest of you also have homework. Join us at the dodgeball game. It should be fun!"

With that, Mr. Quiet lobbed my second egg at me and disappeared down the pole. I caught the egg like a wet fish and managed to put it away before I could accidentally drop it, or before Spork could add it to her scones. As I strolled toward the pole to leave the room, the rest of the class gave me dirty looks and went back to what they were doing. Spork was setting up a turkey fryer, Lenny was reading the paper, Urhiness was in the half-mirror and Snooze, well you know....

"ZZZinkles, thanks for nothing," said Lenny. "Now we have to stay here all night after an already long day."

"You all are staying here? I mean I know Lenny lives here, but the rest of you can go home for a little while before you have to do your homework."

"No, Captain Obvious, we are going back to Laura's to do karaoke and eat chicken tenders," replied Lenny with disgust in his voice.

"Well, then you all could at least think about how we are going to pass fifth grade. If we work together like we did earlier, we might be able to pass." I winked at them and offered a thumbs-up as a sign of encouragement.

"I wouldn't miss seeing you get hit in the head with a red rubber ball for nothing on Earth," said Lenny. "Not to mention, your scrambled egg will be worth the price of admission. I bet Mr. Quiet won't miss on purpose when he sees you as his target."

I turned my thumb up into an "L" (for loser) sign and pointed it toward Lenny. "Lose the attitude, Lenny," I said. Then I gave them the information about the game, slid down the pole, and was out feeling the breeze from the back of Grandma Wilbur's motorcycle before I knew it.

CHAPTER 25

The Wardrobe

"How was school?" asked Grandma Wilbur through the headset we used to communicate while she drove.

"Fine, I guess. I need to go back for night school later on."

"You know you have a game tonight? I hope you have been practicing that special throw I told you about."

"I remember the game. As far as the throw, I almost have it right, but do I have to put on a blind fold and turn my back on the other team?"

She answered, "If you want it to work, you have to trust me."

"Okay, Grandma, but every time I try it I break a window."

"I'm the one who pays for those windows. If you can accidentally hit a window, you can accidentally hit an opponent."

"Alright, I'll try my best. But there's something else that is going to be a problem."

"What is that?" asked Grandma Wilbur.

"I was given an egg and I have to carry it —"

I couldn't even get the sentence through the headset before she interrupted. "Wow, you guys are carrying eggs in elementary! I had to care for an egg in high school. It was fun. I still have my egg."

"Really?" I doubted her because nobody in his or her right mind would keep an egg for that many years.

"Sure do," she said. "I keep it in my jewelry box with my other valuables."

"When did an old egg become valuable?"

"The lessons I learned were valuable. The sacrifice that I went through with that egg gave it value. I also fought in a war with that egg."

"You had a food fight at Laura's, too?"

"No, you silly goat. I went to a real war and fought. I was hungry, but never ate the egg. I treated it like I was holding onto the enemy's prized possession. The enemy tried to blow me up to get to that egg. As you can see, I made it back in one piece. Well, two, if you count the metal plate I have in my head."

We shared a laugh and in no time at all, Grandma Wilbur set the motorcycle on its kickstand. I went to my bedroom and quickly changed into my dodgeball uniform. First, I put on a burnt orange colored pair of spandex shorts. The spandex shorts were so tight they made my toes tingle and restricted the circulation of my blood. Next, I put on my black kneepads that had a skull and crossbones with light up eyes. The uniform's top was a wool sweater with the number thirteen, a hyphen, and then two zeros. The rest of the team considered me unlucky, so they stuck me with thirteen. Not to mention, I had two times zero chance of getting some-body out, so I wore 13-00. I kind of liked my number because it didn't require me to be any good at dodgeball whatsoever.

When I finished putting on my uniform, I started thinking of where to put my egg. If you've ever laid eyes on spandex shorts, then you know that there is no room for hiding anything in them. I wanted to hide the egg in my wool sweater, but the stretched sleeves were too loose and would probably allow the egg to fall out and hit the ground. That's when Grandma Wilbur knocked on my bedroom door.

After inviting Grandma Wilbur into my bedroom, she took one look at me, tossed me a fanny pack, and walked out. A fanny pack. Oh, no!

If you've ever been on vacation, you've seen a fanny pack. A fanny pack is what older people wear to store their belongings. I could be wrong, but I think the fanny part is the strap that wraps around your waist, just above your fanny. The pack portion of the fanny pack covers your stomach and makes you look like a female kangaroo with a joey in her pouch. Folks store glasses with the strings on the arms, prescriptions, pictures, disposable cameras, etc. in their fanny packs. Needless to say, I didn't want to be caught dead wearing a fanny pack, especially with spandex. The only thing about the fanny pack that was close to cool was the fact that the front of it looked a championship belt.

Quickly, I put the thoughts of wearing the fanny pack out of my mind and focused on the fact that I was having some fears about actually going out and playing dodgeball. I mean, I had seen Mr. Quiet's cannon of an arm at Laura's. He was missing on purpose and was still doing damage with the food he was throwing. What would happen if he actually hit someone on purpose? That question was enough to let me know I had to think of something to do in order for me to keep my egg from getting blasted.

After a quick moment, I realized I had to figure out a way to avoid playing in the dodgeball game. Sure, dodgeball was fun, but making it to Knight School alive was more important. Plus, dodging dodgeballs thrown by Mr. Quiet wasn't what I had signed up for. That's when the idea came to my head. Something running around my brain told me to play sick. Everybody knows that when you act sick, you don't have to go where you don't want to.

So, when Grandma Wilbur returned to my room to see if the fanny pack fit, I was holding my stomach and looking at her with a set of the wobbly eyes.

"What's the matter with you?" she asked. I could see in her face that she was thinking about how I was fine just a minute ago.

"I just threw up, Grandma." I was lying and would have no answer if she asked me to produce the bucket that I used for chunk-catching. I was going back to lying to get out of things and I felt pretty guilty about it. Not guilty enough to want to get hit by Mr. Quiet's dodgeball, but still pretty guilty.

CHAPTER 26

The Lie

"I used to do that all the time before I played dodgeball," said Grandma Wilbur, with a big smile. "You'll be fine once you get there." Obviously Grandma Wilbur wasn't going for the sick puppy routine, so I had to scramble, or I was in for it.

"No, Grandma," I explained, "I got sick from school. Mr. Quiet made me order a bunch of nasty food and forced me to do what came natural with it."

"Do you have a phone number for Mr. Quiet?"

"No, but maybe it's in the phonebook."

"Anything else you want me to know?" She looked like she wanted me to lie to her, so I was happy to give her what she wanted. I had to come up with something to help me keep my egg alive until night school started.

"Mr. Quiet burned me in my face with a blow torch to-day. He may have bitten another student's toe and eaten it. He even tried to get a student hit by a bus. He lets one student sleep in class and allows another student to make fun of people all day long. Worst of all, he started a huge food fight at Laura's."

While I was going overboard with the events of the day, my grandmother's ears were up like a Doberman Pinscher. She was starting to sweat a little on her forehead and looked furious, thinking how a teacher could mistreat students. I liked it when she got all riled up and went off on some unsuspecting person. They never had any idea what was coming from her and would crumble under the pressure. Honestly, Grandma Wilbur was an artist when it came to putting other people in their place, and Mr. Quiet was about to be placed.

I gave Grandma Wilbur my saddest, most tortured set of puppy dog eyes and poked my bottom lip out about as far as it could go. I think Grandma Wilbur bought it because she went and looked up Mr. Quiet's telephone number. I could hear her breathing as she flipped through the pages and then dialed the number. Then she pressed the speakerphone button and I could hear the phone ringing.

The phone only rang twice before somebody picked up.

"Quiet residence."

"Is this the residence of Mr. Quiet from Old Endings Preparatory?" asked Grandma Wilbur. She sounded sweeter than a telemarketer who calls when you actually want them to.

"He is I and I am him. Who wants to know?" asked Mr. Quiet.

"This is Wrinkles Wallace's Grandma Wilbur. He was telling me that you forced him to eat some nasty food and now he cannot go to his dodgeball game tonight because his tummy is hurting."

"Poor Wrinkles. I can't believe his tummy is hurting," said Mr. Quiet.

Mr. Quiet was calm. In fact, he was too calm. He either

expected this, or had been through it before. Why did I just lie about him like that?

"Wrinkles also said you burned a student with a torch and nearly had someone run over by a freight train. He said you threw food at people and that you ate people's fingers."

All in all, she wasn't bad. I mean, she did get half of the half-truths I told her correct, so we had a grand total of 25% truth. Twenty-five percent had me excited. I knew I'd be getting out of the dodgeball game, now that my Grandma had turned the mighty Mr. Quiet into Mr. Mute. In my eyes, we were up two-to-nothing on Mr. Quiet, and he was on the ropes.

That was, until he replied, "I believe all the students will be at the dodgeball game tonight. I'll give them all a public apology. That is, if it is okay with you?"

"Fine!" said Grandma Wilbur and she hung up the phone. Her blood pressure and heartbeat must have been up because the veins in her forehead were wiggling. She had defended me with all of her might and I was so proud to have her as my Grandma. Then I realized that Mr. Quiet managed to survive her true wrath by weaseling out with an offer of an apology.

The funny thing about Mr. Quiet was he was so calm on the other end. What was he thinking? I had lied to her and she had lied to him. He didn't even remotely try to defend himself or talk back to her. He just sat there, quietly breathing and listening to her every word. Then he offered up an apology. Something strange was going on and I had a gut feeling that I was in deep, deep T-Rubble. I knew I should have just told the truth, took my egg-cruciating dodgeball beating, and hoped to live to see another day.

Lying was getting me into more and more trouble.

CHAPTER 27

The Clumsy

I was sitting in my room trying to clear my mind when Grandma Wilbur announced, "Wrinkles, it's time to go to your game. Make sure you have your egg in your fanny pack."

I could hear the excitement in her voice. She was fired up about meeting Mr. Quiet at the game to hear him apologize for treating me and my classmates like he did.

"Do I have to go?" I asked. I was trying to get some sympathy from her.

She smiled at me and said, "Yes, you have to go and get your gift. You earned that apology and now you need to go get it. Otherwise, Mr. Quiet might not understand how wrong he was to treat people the way he did. Now, let's go before we keep your sister waiting."

With that, Grandma Wilbur and I met my sister, Clumsy, short for Clumserella, at the motorcycle. Clumsy used to ride between Grandma and me until she passed out due to the lack of oxygen getting to her body. We didn't know we were sandwiching her, let alone cutting off her respiratory system. If it weren't for us somehow doing CPR whenever Grandma Wilbur and I bumped into Clumsy when we landed from jumps, and the 100 mile per hour winds filling Clumsy's lungs, she could have died.

After the CPR scare, Grandma Wilbur thought of a better place for Clumsy to ride. No, Grandma Wilbur did not spend the money to get a sidecar for her motorcycle for Clumsy. Instead, Grandma Wilbur tied a rope around Clumsy's waist and allowed her to skate behind us on rollerblades. She even gave Clumsy some ski poles to help her keep her balance. Honestly, Clumsy normally falls a lot, but she never cries or complains. She's a trooper because not many people can handle rollerblading behind the motorcycle at speeds in excess of 150 miles per hour. I mean, I survived it. Grandma Wilbur trained both of us very well. And, when it became evident that Clumsy wasn't as good at balancing as I was, Grandma Wilbur protected her by ordering her a full body cast. Indeed, nothing says *I love you* like writing it on a plastered cast in permanent marker.

In no time, we all took our positions on and behind the motorcycle and were off to the game. When we finally arrived at the gym, there was some good news and some bad news. The good news was my sister had only fallen once. I was very proud of her. The bad news was that she had fallen coming out of our driveway and was dragged the entire trip. Once Grandma Wilbur applied the kickstand, I climbed off the bike and removed my helmet. Grandma Wilbur went to the back of the bike, picked up Clumsy, and duct-taped her body cast back together. She then unhooked the rope from the bike and used it to pull her along. As always, Clumsy never said a word.

As we walked through the main doors of the gym, we could hear what sounded like rhythmic explosions. Instantly, I was terrified. I thought a bazooka was going off every couple of seconds. Grandma Wilbur was battle-tested, so the sounds didn't bother her at all. She was too busy trying to get her and Clumsy some snacks before the game, to really care what was going on. When I finally did get a chance to see what was making this horrendous sound, I almost fainted.

CHAPTER 28

The Gym

The sound of dangerous doom was Mr. Quiet throwing the red rubber balls at the wall and they were nearly exploding upon contact. The blocks that made up the wall were starting to crumble and create small piles of rock chips. Mr. Quiet was no joke with a dodgeball in his hand. Upon *checking* the dangerous scene, I saw my teammates scattered around the gymnasium, lying motionless on the ground, as if they weren't living anymore. Even though I could see their chests going up and down, I yelled back in the hallway for Grandma Wilbur to *call* 911. I hoped they would be able to get some medical *care* before long. (Check-Call-Care -- Yeah, that's First-Aid.) That's if Mr. Quiet would even allow the paramedics to come onto the court to help, or if they would risk their own lives to save the wounded.

The whispers from the audience in the stands let me know that the entire incident happened because my team-mates played a practice game of one-man dodgeball with Mr. Quiet. The only rules were: every man for himself, and the person with the ball could only take five steps before throwing the ball. Mr. Quiet had suckered them in with his small size and tricked them into thinking he couldn't play. It didn't take long for him to paralyze my entire team because he obviously wasn't missing on purpose anymore. This must have been what he meant by warming up his arm for later.

Lenny brought me out of my trance when he ran over my foot with his wheelchair and said, "It sucks to be you."

I looked at him and a tear started to well up in my right eye. Before it could fall, the referee walked up to me and asked, "Do you have a team of five?"

I tried to dodge the question by asking, "Does he have a team of five?"

"He has a team of one, and when you see him play, you'll know exactly why."

"My team is over there." I pointed to my teammates who looked like crashed cars at a junk yard.

"They cannot play," said the referee. "The ambulance will be here to get them within the next hour."

I sighed and hid my egg-saving delight. "Well, I guess we won't —"

Lenny inhaled and fake-sneezed the word, "Loser."

I stuttered and looked at Lenny. "Well, well, I guess I'll have to get my other starting four." I pointed to my classmates and they had looks of horror in their eyes. They instantly went from being happy, since they were about to see me get blasted in exchange for giving them night school, to feeling like they were going to be using their health insurance tonight. Needless to say, they were not happy with me.

CHAPTER 29

The Pieces

While walking back to the bleachers to talk to my team, I noticed Grandma Wilbur walking into the gym with some snacks in her hand. She was also pulling Clumsy by the rope still wrapped around her waist. When Grandma Wilbur stopped and sat on the end of the bleachers, she didn't realize the rope had some slack in it, or that Clumsy's momentum caused her to keep rollerblading onto the court. I guess anything on the court was an opponent in Mr. Quiet's eyes, thus making what he did to Clumsy fair game. Mr. Quiet fired the ball at her and yelled, "Strrrrrrrike!" like she was a bowling pin.

As soon as the ball made contact with Clumsy, the entire body cast burst into a thousand little pieces. There was dust and debris all over the place. I was afraid for Clumsy. Especially after the dust settled and nothing else was left. I thought her body must have broken into millions of tiny pieces. My tears started rolling down my cheeks and soon I was crying like a baby. Mr. Quiet had killed my sister. My sister!

That's when Grandma Wilbur walked up chewing on Sour Boppers and dragging the rope. She whispered in my ear, "Wrinkles, Clumsy's gone."

"I know that, Grandma." There was no way I could hold back the emotions I was feeling. Yet, I did notice that Grandma Wilbur wasn't even crying or upset.

She kept chewing her Soup Boppers until she paused to say, "Wrinkles, you don't understand. Clumsy left years ago and I didn't know how to tell you. She moved to Las Vegas and is now a casino developer. I know I should have told you earlier, but –"

I looked my Grandma in her eyes and asked, "So she didn't *just* die?" My tears had instantly stopped rolling and I was very quickly returning back to normal.

"No, she didn't."

"Well, then we've got a game to play," I said. "Come on, Knights. The Spork-food smell of revenge is in the air!"

At that point, I'm not sure if I was overly happy that Clumsy didn't just get blown into smithereens, or perhaps I had a memory lapse. I soon came to my senses and realized that I had made a mistake. Mr. Quiet had been warming up his arm for the real game when he took his anger out on my old teammates. My new teammates and I were in some serious trouble.

I kept asking myself, "Why did I lie about him?" To top it off he was giving us that eerie smile of his. It was the kind of smile that someone who just broke his arm would give you if you made him pause from the pain to say "CHEESE" and take a happy picture. This was the kind of cheese that Spork would put on her grilled cheese sandwiches.

A buzzer rang in the background and the referee asked for the team captains to come to center court. As I walked to center court I noticed that the paramedics must have rescued my old teammates while I was talking to Grandma Wilbur. Then I saw the janitor of the gym sweeping the remains of Clumsy's cast off the court. Mr. Quiet met me at center court and we stood there looking each other in the eyes. Of course, his head was leaned back and my chin was scraping my sternum enough to make me feel like I had a double chin.

"Both teams need to protect themselves at all times," said the referee. "If you get knocked down, you have 10 seconds to get up, or you will likely be hit again. If you make it to the sidelines, you cannot be hit again. Do you have any questions, gentlemen?"

"Yeah, I have a question," I said. "Aren't those the rules for a boxing match?"

"The first team that gets here can add a few rules to the game. If you had arrived before he did, this game could have been more like synchronized swimming."

"I have a comment," said Mr. Quiet as he turned toward the audience. He cleared his throat and said, "I'd like to extend my warmest apologies to my entire class for my behavior today. I realize that I was truly wrong."

Mr. Quiet was lying through his missing teeth. My grandma clapped and smiled as she gave him an *I-know-that's-right* look. Meanwhile, I turned to join my newest teammates on the black line. They looked like they wanted to run and hide under the bleachers. What had I gotten us into?

CHAPTER 30

The Game

At the start of a dodgeball game, five rubber dodgeballs are placed on the middle line of the court. When the whistle blows, the teams race to get the balls and then throw them at the opposing team. No player can cross the middle line or they are automatically out. When you are out, you cannot return to the game unless somebody on your team catches the opponent's ball. If you do catch the opponent's ball, then they are out. When everybody on your team is out, you lose the game. When you add those rules to the ones Mr. Quiet had us using, you pretty much get how a game of dodgeball should be played. Sure, there might be a few more rules, but that's all I remember my teammates telling me.

When the referee blew the whistle, I was the only one on my team who moved. The rest stood there like statues because they were scared of getting hit. Mr. Quiet managed to get three of the balls safely to his side while I ran and got one. Then, Urhiness backpedaled toward the line while using her mirror as a guide and picked up a ball. The referee whistled and called her out for crossing the line. She would be of no help because that mirror had defeated her again. In her frustration, Urhiness kicked the ball in our direction and it went toward Lenny. Amazingly, he caught the ball in his lap and seemed to be ready.

Mr. Quiet put one dodgeball inside the back of his shirt and another in the front. He slowly started walking toward the center line. He looked like he had on a double deluxe fanny pack himself. He flicked the third ball back and forth between his hands in a controlled and playful manner. We could tell he was simply toying with us.

Mr. Quiet walked toward the center line, looked at my fanny pack, and threw the ball at Spork. My first reaction was to jump and spread my legs in hopes that the ball would fly through where my legs had been and completely miss me. Good thing his tricky eyes were a false alarm for me. Spork wasn't so lucky.

As the ball moved toward her, it seemed like it was traveling in slow motion. Spork tried to move out of the way, but the ball was a heat-seeking GPS missile heading in her direction. As Spork turned to run, the ball grazed her thigh. Spork fell to the ground and red stuff appeared on her leg.

Spork started screaming in agony, "He hit me! I can't feel my leg! I can't feel my leg! Call an ambulance! I'm bleeding! Please don't let them cut off my leg on the operating table!"

I made my way over to Spork, who was cringing and crying while in obvious pain. I could see why the red stuff on her leg made her feel like she needed immediate medical attention. I moved my head closer to her wound when I had a thought. I knew I wasn't losing my mind when I smelled the faint scent of tomato.

I asked, "Do you have ketchup packets in your pocket?"

"What good cooks don't keep ketchup packets in their pocket? Stop asking silly questions and get me to a doctor!"

I shook my head in frustration. "That's not blood, that's ketchup!"

Spork kept screaming, "Mr. Quiet hit me!"

Before Mr. Quiet thought Spork was begging for seconds, or a double dose of dodgeball dessert, I helped her to the sideline. I couldn't believe we were already down two players.

As soon as Spork sat down, Mr. Quiet sent thunder and lightning at Lenny. Lenny moved his wheelchair clockwise and the ball hit the side of his chair. It bent the wheel and made Lenny's side impact airbags go off. I didn't even realize that those new wheelchairs came standard with airbags. The way the blast rocked the wheelchair, I knew Lenny would be filing an insurance claim on his totaled out wheelchair. That is, if, and only if, he made it out alive. I managed to push Lenny over to a safe zone behind the bleachers.

Mr. Quiet's next target was Snooze. Snooze was propped up in the corner of the back wall. A flying ball of fire was thrown toward Snooze and it hit him in the chest. The ball rolled back to Mr. Quiet's side and Snooze didn't move. When the ten-count ended, Mr. Quiet was able to fire again, and he did. This bombing on Snooze went on every ten seconds for about an hour. While Mr. Quiet was definitely losing some of the power in his throwing arm, he still had his accuracy.

After the sixty minutes ended, I had already replaced Lenny's busted wheel with his spare. I held up the old wheel to show Lenny that the ball Mr. Quiet threw actually never hit him. Even though Lenny was still technically in the game, he was hesitant to go back on the court. During the 3,600 seconds that Snooze was being bombarded, I did everything I could to talk Lenny out of being afraid of getting hit by Mr. Quiet. I reminded him of how the coffee at Laura's had spilled on his leg and he did not feel a thing. I let him know that if Mr. Quiet was throwing really hard, then Snooze would be wide awake and screaming by now. I also let Lenny know that he wouldn't be out if Mr. Quiet hit him in the face with the ball.

Lenny responded, "Tell my handsome face that getting hit by a brick doesn't count."

I replied, "Lenny, Mr. Quiet knows he can't hit you in the face. His only chance of getting you out is hitting you in the chest or the legs."

"Great! All I have to worry about is broken ribs, separated shins, or a crushed calf," said Lenny.

"Look, just go out there and distract Mr. Quiet so I can hit him and end the game."

Lenny gave me a look that let me know he really didn't want to be a damaged decoy, but that he was willing to see if I would hit or be hit. I think Lenny was ready for this game to be over and so were the rest of us.

With a push from me, Lenny rolled back onto the court and distracted Mr. Quiet just enough to temporarily stop Snooze from absorbing more punishment. That's when Mr. Quiet's dodgeball bomb came toward Lenny's head. Either Lenny was scared or he had skills with his wheelchair. Lenny pushed his arms forward on the rear wheels of his wheelchair and managed to pop an awesome wheelie that allowed him to keep disaster and damage away from his dentures. With

Lenny's feet now where his head used to be, Mr. Quiet reloaded and fired another dodgeball that blasted Lenny's left ankle and caused him to do a backflip in the wheelchair. Lenny stuck a perfect landing, but he was still out. Good thing he was wearing his seatbelt or things could have really ended badly.

At that moment, I ran from behind the bleachers to do the backwards throw the way Grandma Wilbur had taught me. I had just managed to get the blindfold on when the referee finished the ten-count. I hadn't even raised my arm to throw the ball when I was directly hit on the fanny pack by Mr. Quiet's dodgeball. It was obvious that he was trying to kill two birds with one stone by getting me out and crushing my egg. I wanted to cry and argue, but the referee blew the whistle and ordered me off the court before someone slipped and hurt themselves on my tears. While walking to the sideline, I didn't even want to look inside the fanny pack because I knew my egg was in that big omelet up in the sky.

Once I took a seat next to my teammates, I realized that we were going to lose. All we had left was Snooze, and he was asleep. Mr. Quiet was going to continue to blast him with the dodgeballs until I threw in the forfeit towel.

I was just about to call it quits when my Grandma Wilbur said, "Wrinkles, even a garbage can will eventually get a steak."

She was right. All I had to do was keep waiting for Snooze to turn into a garbage can and he could get us that winning steak. The next three shots were almost too brutal to watch because Mr. Quiet was pelting Snooze's torso, legs, and arms. This was a one-sided boxing match and Mr. Quiet was pummeling Snooze.

As Mr. Quiet threw the fourth flying comet at Snooze, the miracle happened. Snooze was starting to fall and ended up sitting on his rear. The ball that was meant to make his knees buckle had actually caught him in his chest area. Snooze leaned over at the perfect time and trapped the dodgeball between his legs and chest.

Snooze had caught the ball and got the steak! The crowd of ten went crazy. Lenny actually got up and did a little dance before he realized it. Mr. Quiet was now an official two-time loser. We had beaten him with his own rules.

When the crowd calmed down, Mr. Quiet made his announcement. "You beat me, fair and square. Now, if you don't get to class in ten minutes, you'll be late and detention will be in the dungeon with the lion."

"But, I didn't eat anything for dinner," said Urhiness.

"Don't worry, Urhiness. I'm sure Spork will have something for everyone to eat. That's your assignment for tonight. Knights, you all must eat a meal prepared by Spork."

Spork smiled. Everyone else lost their appetite. I lowered my head and thought about the nastiness of having to eat a meal prepared by Spork. I'd rather eat vegetables than nibble on Spork's horrendous concoctions.

Suddenly, my eyes focused on the fanny pack and the horror that was sure to be inside. I had to open the fanny pack, but I knew that failure and shelled yolk would be there. Not to mention, Spork would surely be trying to scoop the mess out to make dinner. Mr. Quiet looked at me and gave me that eerie smile of his before he walked out of the gym. Even in defeat, he was setting himself up to win later on.

CHAPTER 31

The Crack

After Mr. Quiet left the gym, the strangest thing happened. For a second I thought my stomach was going crazy over the thought of having to eat Spork's meal. As I put my hand on my stomach, I heard a tiny crack coming from the fanny pack. Then I realized the stomach issue wasn't a stomach issue. I reached for the zipper and felt some movement. It couldn't be what I thought it was. I unzipped the fanny pack and wasn't ready for what I saw when I looked into the eyes of a baby chick. It was feathery and cute, and would be dinner if Spork found out about it.

How was I going to hide this feathered friend of mine from Mr. Quiet?

How did the little chick live through the blast from Mr. Quiet?

Grandma Wilbur saw the look on my face and said, "That fanny pack is shaped like a championship belt for a reason. I lined it with thin, lightweight armor. It is bullet proof, sound proof to exterior noise, weather resistant, and sure to withstand the puny arm of young Sittin' B. Quiet. How do you think I made it through the war without breaking my egg? Now, come on before you're late."

On our motorcycle ride to Old Endings Preparatory I realized my only real concern was keeping the chick quiet so the others wouldn't know that I had a living animal with me. I wanted to stop by the store and get some duct tape for the chick's beak before I entered the school, but Grandma Wilbur refused to stop. Once we arrived at school, she reached into her pocket and pulled out some Yummy Gummy Worms for the chick to eat.

"Here you go, Wrinkles," said Grandma Wilbur.

"Grandma Wilbur, birds eat *real* worms."

Grandma Wilbur replied, "These Yummy Gummy Worms are worms and if the chick is hungry, then they're better than nothing."

"I guess you're right,"

"Guess? You guess I'm right? Wrinkles, I know I'm right! Since you're into guessing, guess what time it is?

"Knight time?" I answered while asking a question.

"It sure is. It's time for you to go in there and KNOW you're going to pass fifth grade. I'll pick you up in the morning."

When Grandma Wilbur zoomed away on her motorcycle, I fed a Yummy Gummy Worm to the chick and it quieted down. Either that or the beak was stuck together. I looked over at Laura's and noticed some movement inside that made me nervous, so I hurried inside the school.

Moments later, I made it to the rope at Old Endings Preparatory and managed to avoid the lion before the evening tardy bell rang. By the time I was eye level with the floor of the classroom, I could see my classmates were already seated and fuming that I got them into this mess. Because of me, we had been in a food fight, a dodgeball war, and now we had to eat Spork's cooking while going to school late at night. Even though I was trying to help us all pass, things weren't working out as I had planned, and there was a good chance that Mr. Quiet still thought we were losers.

"Krinkles, you do know that you are going to replace my damaged wheelchair," said Lenny. He was looking at me with those beady eyes again.

I replied, "You do know you stood up and danced in the gym. Maybe that shot to your foot was helpful. Maybe the flip you did helped to turn your leg switch back to the 'ON' position. Plus, I know you have it insured." I smiled and hoped that would be enough to get him to look on the bright side. It wasn't.

Lenny asked, "What about my dentures after tonight's meal?"

"We can get you some new ones and use your old ones for wood chips on the playground. Don't worry."

"Cut the cheese, Wrinkles," said Spork. "You're the main reason your old dodgeball team is in the hospital right now. Look how you dragged us into your issues and got my leg nearly amputated by Doctor Dodgeball. Snooze's meat is so tender, it would fall off the bone if I cooked it. Lenny's airbags went off. We're here for night school —"

I knew she was going to go on forever so I had to stop her. "And you are going to cook us the greatest meal ever! I'm so hungry I could eat whatever you decide is good, Spork." I had another one of my lapses in judgment where I let my mouth go faster than my brain and it was going to punish my stomach before the night was over.

Spork smiled.

"But you lied about Mr. Quiet," said Urhiness. "He recorded the conversation with him and your Grandma Wilbur and played it for us before you got to the gym. How can you look at yourself in the mirror knowing that you lied about him?"

"You're right, Miss Reflection Specialist. I did ruin the trust that we are trying to establish. I did lie, and that was wrong. I'll spill the beans to my grandma later on. I was trying to protect my egg from getting cracked."

"I'm sure it isn't recognizable anymore," replied Urhiness.

Lenny added, "Mirror, mirror in her hand, saw you got hit by a boulder, man. Mirror, mirror stay out of her hand, lying is bad, make Wrinkles understand."

"You got that right," I said. "It isn't eggs-actly recognizable anymore."

Lucky for me, Snooze was asleep and I wouldn't have to explain any of his injuries to him. That would take some smooth-talking because I could tell he was in tremendous pain. His snores were sounding more like "ouch" than "oink."

Before long, Mr. Quiet climbed into the classroom. Nobody said a word. He didn't look like his normal self. He was wearing pajamas that made him look like a lumpy, gray bunny with a dirty cotton tail and ears that lopped over like thirsty house plants. Obviously, Mr. Quiet's pajamas had been through better days.

Mr. Quiet sat down at his desk, opened up a drawer, removed a camouflage sleeping bag and a fat pillow with a matching camouflage case. He opened up another desk drawer, took out some chocolate chip cookies, and poured a glass of milk. This didn't look like his first time teaching here at night. When he finally broke the silence, we were all shocked.

Mr. Quiet said, "Knights of Night School, this is our first session. I am so happy to be here." He gave us another sarcastic face that let us know he didn't mean a word he said. He continued, "As you all know, your assignment for tonight is to eat a meal prepared by Spork. Once this meal goes down your throat, it is not allowed to come back up, or else she fails. Everyone must eat the entire meal and Spork must cook it. I've notified all local businesses not to deliver anything to the school or the surrounding area. Under no circumstances are you to wake me during my relentless pursuit of rest."

Lenny said, "You need to get as much beauty sleep as you can because —"

Urhiness cleared her throat to hush Lenny before he could say something that would get him into more trouble.

"While I'm getting my beauty sleep, Lenny will be the Garçon," said Mr. Quiet. "You are to serve the food with a smile. If you are impolite, you fail. Urhiness, you will be the hostess. You will arrange the meal and escort everybody to their table in the back. You must look your customers in the eye. You cannot use your mirror, or you will fail."

The way things were going, I was starting to think Snooze and I were going to slide by without having much responsibility. Boy, was I wrong.

Mr. Quiet continued, "Snooze is a customer at the restaurant. He must eat! Wrinkles, you are also a food critic for the Old Endings Observer, so you have to write an article for the paper. Since you are also going to be a competitive chef, you have to cook the same meal as Spork. Everyone is to eat both of the meals. You two will be preparing chicken noodle soup for starters, lasagna for the main course, and That Stuff for dessert. The ingredients are on the paper that Urhiness will pass out."

Urhiness walked up to Mr. Quiet's desk and was given two pieces of paper, just as Mr. Quiet had promised.

Before we could look at the papers, Mr. Quiet went on, "Spork and Wrinkles need to go to the grocery store and get the ingredients. Nobody else is allowed to leave the building. When I wake up in the morning, I will know exactly who won the cooking contest. Wrinkles, I'm sure your meal will be better, so you can only win if your egg is still intact. Also, don't forget that article. Spork, do the *best* you can. Morning starts at 12:00 a.m. and I'll be up after that. Oh, and by the way, Snooze must be awake to eat. Spork and Wrinkles, touch cooking mitts, and come out cooking."

He smiled. I was doomed. If Spork saw my chick, it would be the main ingredient in her soup. Even though I was sure to win the cooking contest, my egg also had to survive the recipes. I could see this going bad before we even started and I realized I had to do something about it. How could we get Lenny to be a polite waiter, Urhiness away from her mirror, Snooze to wake up and eat, and Spork to beat me in cooking? That was a lot of lightning striking in the same place. Just then, the fanny pack started to quiver. I heard a chirp and instantly raised my hand to try to cover it up.

Mr. Quiet called on me. "Wrinkles, do you have something to say?"

"May I come to your desk?"

"After you give your fanny pack to Spork, you can come up to my desk."

"But I don't want anything to happen to my egg."

"Do as I say, Wrinkles. You can trust Spork, can't you?"

The chick was going to be my noodle soup nightmare because if Spork heard even a peep out of it, there would be serious consequences. On my way to Spork's area, I realized that since Snooze was snoring louder than normal, perhaps it lowered Spork's chances of hearing the chick. I tilted Snooze's chin toward his chest and his snoring volume instantly went up a few more notches. When I made it over to Spork, I put the fanny pack as far away from her as possible, but she didn't notice it because she had her back turned while looking at some cookbooks.

When I arrived at Mr. Quiet's desk, he gave me that crazy smile again.

He asked, "How can I help you, Wrinkles?"

I whispered, "I had an issue with the egg you gave me."

"Yeah, I figured you would. You broke it."

"No, I didn't break it. See, my egg isn't an egg anymore. After you hit me with the dodgeball in the fanny pack, things changed and the egg hatched into a chickadee."

"Tell me something I don't know." Mr. Quiet gave me a coy smile and shook his head at me.

"You knew and you still gave it to me?" I asked.

"After seeing how you handled that little situation at Laura's, I figured you were ready for more responsibility. Anybody can keep an egg from cracking, but can you raise a baby chicken around a barnyard animal hunter like Spork?"

"You tried to crush my egg with that shot to the fanny pack."

"You tried to get me fired by lying to your grandma about what happened at school today."

I said, "I'm sorry for lying," loud enough for the class to hear me.

"As you should be, Wrinkles, and I fully accept your apology," replied Mr. Quiet so everyone could hear. Then he returned to his whisper and said, "By the way, I knew your grandmother's fanny pack would be able to withstand the blow. Wrinkles, just make sure the chick makes it through the night and you'll pass fifth grade. The rest of your classmates will be here for a while because they cannot get over their issues. Urhiness is mesmerized by that mirror, Lenny just doesn't know when to stop talking, Snooze won't be awake, and you already know that Spork's food is double-nasty deluxe. She'll never get the restaurant of her dreams if she cannot figure out how to cook for her customers."

"Mr. Quiet, I feel like I might be the unofficial leader here, so I can't just leave them."

"Wrinkles, some leaders lead by example. So, when you pass, it'll show them that they can pass. I'll admit, your classmates are getting better, but I see no reason to make someone as smart as you wait on them before they finally get the clue."

Mr. Quiet's return to dunking his cookies into the milk and eating the soggy creation meant our conversation was over. I smiled at him to show I agreed, but I had to keep myself from going off on him. I knew my classmates were quirky, but we could all pass if we worked together. I couldn't believe Mr. Quiet was trying to separate me from my fellow Knights, especially when I felt we needed each other most.

I left Mr. Quiet's desk and went to get my fanny pack from Spork's area. She was still so focused on looking through her cookbooks for tonight's recipes, I didn't have to worry so much about leaving it there all that time. I walked back to my seat while trying to ignore how pleasant Mr. Quiet had been about me getting out of fifth grade. No more of this nonsense, I thought, back to my pizza delivering days. Then I forced myself to think about how I was going to solve this puzzle that had just been presented.

The chick interrupted my thinking with a noise that I had to play off as a hiccup. Spork sprung to attention. She must have been some sort of chicken hawk because as soon as she heard the squeak, she ran around with her arms spread out, as if she was soaring. She had the fly swatter spatula in one hand and an oven mitt on the other. I kept acting like I had the hiccups and hoped she wouldn't flatten my poor, little chick.

Meanwhile, Mr. Quiet started yawning, stretching, and rubbing his eyes. He managed to get comfortable on the floor and quickly fell asleep after a few minutes of tossing and turning. If he was like most kids, then all we had to worry about was if our little, innocent-looking monster would sleep through the night.

CHAPTER 32

The Menu

I gathered the troops around me and we looked over the menu. The lasagna needed to be cooked for about two hours and That Stuff needed to either be cooled in the refrigerator for four hours, or be in the freezer for two. The soup could be done rather quickly, but I had to keep Spork away from my chick in order to pass. The ingredients for our meals were:

The Soup

Chicken
Chicken Broth
Noodles

The Lasagna

Ground Beef
Sweet Turkey Sausage
Pepperoni
Sharp Cheddar Cheese

Mozzarella Cheese
Mild Cheddar Cheese
Tomato Sauce
Lasagna Noodles

That Stuff

Graham Crackers
Butter
Strawberry Cream Cheese
Pineapple Cream Cheese
Confectioner's Sugar
Bananas
Crushed Pineapple
Strawberries
Whipped Cream
Maraschino Cherries

I took one look at the filthy kitchen and knew there was no way we'd get any good ingredients from there. Even if we did have all of the ingredients we would need, we'd have horrible results just from the pans and plates we needed to cook with. They were coated with old nastiness. I walked over to Spork's area and started running hot water in the sink. I added some bleach, a half bottle of dish soap, and some dirty dishes before I spoke to Urhiness.

I said, "Urhiness, we're leaving you in charge of Spork's kitchen."

"Oh no, you're not leaving Urhiness in charge of *my* kitchen!" yelled Spork. Her oven mitt was instantly on her hip and she waved her spatula at me.

"She's in charge of seeing herself in the dishwater and on the dishes. Plus, you and I need to get to the store in a hurry, or we won't be able to finish in time."

Before Spork could reply, Urhiness smiled and declared, "Yes! I get to make these plates shine like mirrors!"

I mimed an act of washing dishes so that Spork would get my point. Once she did, of course she had no problems with that. After all, washing dishes was one thing Spork hated to do.

Then I turned to Lenny and said, "Lenny, you're in charge of making sure all of the plates are shiny enough. If they are not, you have to point out all of the stains to Urhiness. When she finishes washing the plates, you are in charge of drying them off, so they don't get streaks. Then, take the wet towel and put it on Snooze's neck, to try to wake him up. Oh, and try to work together. Decorate or something."

I guess Lenny was okay with the plan because he did not have anything smart to say. Maybe it was because he could point out what was wrong with the dishes without getting into any trouble for making fun of Urhiness. Maybe he was happy he could get Snooze wet without it being a bad thing.

With everyone having something to do, Spork and I slid down the fireman's pole. When I landed, I accidently fell on the fanny pack, but I could still feel the chick moving around. A second later I heard a chick-noise coming from the fanny pack. The only thing that stopped Spork from searching me was that I acted like my shoes were squeaking on the dry floor. She looked at me, but before she could ask a question I said, "I wish my shoes would quit squeaking."

"Wrinkles, that sounded more like a squawk than a squeak. Are you sure that wasn't squawking because —"

I quickly changed the subject by asking, "Are we walking or are you driving?

"Without a doubt!" answered Spork. She showed me her keys and we walked out of the front door of the school.

CHAPTER 33

The Drive

Once we were out of the school and outside in the darkness, I was happy to see that Laura's was closed for the evening. It looked like they had started building some sort of war machine to get back at us tomorrow. As we walked toward the school's nearly empty parking lot, I saw Spork push the automatic start button for her vehicle. I heard the sound of a twerp-twerp and the engine starting. A few more steps and I realized Spork drove an ice cream truck. That's when I knew that things were going to get even more interesting.

Spork's ice cream truck was crazy! It sat really low to the ground, so it surely had issues with speed bumps. She had big, shiny chrome rims and the paint glittered at night. The sign on the passenger side read, "Spork's L.O. Ice Cream." If the L.O. in her sign didn't stand for "Leftovers," blended and frozen in cups and then re-named "Ice Cream," Spork would have had a line of customers following her like zombies. But just one taste of those cups and people plugged their ears and covered their mouths when she drove around, looking to lure customers.

After putting on sunglasses and her seatbelt, Spork said, "Wrinkles, you better buckle up."

She didn't have to tell me twice. I already made a habit of wearing my seatbelt every time I got into a vehicle. I did it for safety and because it's the law.

Spork turned up the music and was blasting the same song I remembered ice cream trucks playing when they drove through my neighborhood, except this song was much louder. The bass had my chest hurting, but I was sure that the soundproofing from the exterior of my fanny pack was keeping my chick okay. Next, Spork turned on the lights and a disco ball started spinning. Then she flipped this special switch and the truck bounced up in the air. She even had hydraulics on this ice cream truck! A couple more switches later and we were hopping and swaying from side to side like a nervous bullfrog.

Before we could get out of the parking lot, I found out that the only thing worse than Spork's cooking was her driving. Oh boy! The tires screeched and we jumped the curb before we officially made it to the street. At that point, things were getting crazier by the minute.

We made a right on Michigan Avenue and headed west. Apparently, Spork's glasses made her color blind because she obviously couldn't tell the difference between the red, yellow, and green lights. She just kept going, as if she didn't have any brakes. Cars and trucks all around us were swerving and crashing while we traveled toward the grocery store. By the time we made it to Ellsworth and veered right, we were doing about a hundred miles per hour. The truck was hopping up and down on the front wheels. The hopping made my view out of the windshield go from looking at the moon and big dipper, to seeing cars ahead of us swerving to get out of the way. With all of the loud music, lights reflecting off the disco ball, and high speed, the other motorists must have thought we were an undercover ambulance. I kept trying to tell her to slow down, but the music was too loud.

I was a nervous wreck when we finally pulled into the grocery store's parking lot. The place was called Forgotten Food. The large neon sign had GARDEN-GOTTEN FOOD written in capital letters, but some of the letters' lights were blown, so the sign actually read, --R----OTTEN FOOD. And this is where Spork wanted to get the ingredients for our dinner.

When we got closer to the actual store, Spork turned down the stereo and I was finally able to ask, "Aren't you going to park in the back, so you don't get any dents in your truck from the carts?"

"Are you crazy? People over there swing their doors open and damage cars too. I have a special parking space."

It didn't take long to realize what Spork meant when she hit another switch and dropped the truck so low to the ground, the metal created sparks. If that wasn't crazy enough, she actually drove the ice cream truck through the double sliding doors of the store and parked near the fruits and vegetables. We unbuckled our seat belts and got out. Spork pushed the button on her keychain, activated her alarm, and waited for me to get a shopping cart.

CHAPTER 34

The Store

As I walked to get the shopping cart, the greeter at the store smiled at me. She had to be at least seventy-five years old. She had a gray smock and shiny silver hair. Honestly, she looked like she would be a hot date for Lenny.

She asked, "How are you, Wrinkles?"

I looked at her name tag and replied, "I'm fine, Agnes. How do you know my name?"

"Mr. Quiet told me a week ago that I should be expecting you two."

"He sure is a thorough young man." I had just met the guy this morning and he already knew I'd be here a week ago. Mr. Quiet was no slouch in the planning department. I reached for a cart when Agnes spoke again.

"Wrinkles, it is store policy to check our customers' bags when they bring them into the store."

I was nervous by now. I know Spork was wondering what was taking so long, so she walked over to see what was going on. I said, "It's just a fanny pack."

"Wrinkles, I still have to take a look," said Agnes. "Mr. Quiet, umm, I mean, the store manager, said to check out all fanny packs, too."

I shook my head in disbelief because this would be the first step toward making my chick walk the chicken soup plank. I unzipped the fanny pack as Spork looked through some coupons that Agnes had given her. Agnes had to put her glasses on to see what was in the bag. When she peered in, the chick let off a little chirp that I thought for sure was going to have it swimming in noodle soup before the night was over.

"Oh, what a pretty, feathered animal," mumbled Agnes, before she turned to greet the next group of customers. I could not believe she blew my cover. She could have just looked at the chick without saying a word.

Spork practically attacked me like a wildcat. "Feathered animal? What, like a bird? Wrinkles, do you have a bird in there?!!! I bet it tastes like chicken! Yeah, CHICKEN NOODLE SOUP, here we come!" She started dancing and smiling.

"No, Spork, I have a leather sandal in here. Who with more than half a brain would carry around a feathered animal?" I asked.

"Stop lying, Wrinkles. When you lie, your forehead gets those wrinkle lines in it. Where do you think you got your name from?"

One of my life's mysteries had just been solved, but that opened up another can of worms. Spork knew I had a chick in the fanny back. With some hesitation, I finally said, "Yeah, I have a bird in here, but you can't have it."

"What kind?" Spork demanded to know.

"It's a baby chick."

"CHICKEN! We can put it in the soup!" The other customers were looking at us funny.

"I'm afraid not," I said. "Spork, the chick is allergic to starch."

"Wrinkles, we're not ironing its feathers, we're going to cook it in the soup!"

I worked on keeping my forehead wrinkles from bouncing up and down like her ice cream truck when I said, "The noodles in the soup have starch and I don't want the chick getting sick and throwing up in the soup. Otherwise, Mr. Quiet might end up failing us both."

"Whatever, Wrinkles. Don't insult my intelligence. You want me to be dumb enough to think that a chick can be allergic to starch. To pass, I need to cook, and chicken is on the menu," said Spork, fully intent on putting my chick on the chopping block.

"I'm sorry, Spork. You are absolutely right. Chicken is on the menu, just not *this* chicken."

"That little chirper of yours better watch its hind feathers."

"Spork, take this cart. You get the stuff on your list and I'll get mine. We'll meet back here in ten minutes."

From there we split up. I jogged through the aisles and ended up with all of my ingredients in about five minutes. It would have taken less time, but I kept weaving through all of the younger kids who were out at the store with their parents at this time of night. The kids looked like zombies. Didn't they have to go to school the next day?

As I made my way back to the meeting spot, I saw three men crowding around Spork. I came closer and was able to make out the conversation.

"I didn't steal the grapes," claimed Spork. She looked nervous. Her hands were shaking like a pair of hot dice at a casino.

"Ma'am," said the undercover security guard in charge. "We saw you eating the grapes and giving them away. That is considered stealing."

He was about ready to put the cuffs on her when I tried my best to step in and help.

I said, "Sir, she isn't a thief, and we are meeting right here to pay for the grapes and everything else in our carts. Besides, she hasn't even left the store yet."

Spork added, "That's not stealing. I do it all the time. The sign said 'Buy 1, Get 1 free,' so I'm eating the free one."

"I'd advise you not to do so anymore," said the security guard. "Grape eating before grape paying is considered stealing."

Spork replied, "You sound serious. Let me get this straight, eating the grapes is stealing?"

"Yes, it sure is, and you can be arrested and sent to jail for it," answered the security guard.

"I'll have to tell my mother," said Spork. "She eats grapes at every store she goes to. She always told me that you can sample a few grapes to see if they taste good enough to buy."

The security guard gave Spork a stern look and said, "Our store does not consider any of our grapes to be samples. I'm going to let you off with a strict warning this time. If I ever see you eating food in the store without a receipt, I'm going to have to arrest you."

Spork smiled in appreciation and we both were relieved. I thought for sure she was going to jail for a really long time.

Once the security guard left, we went to the self-scan to

check out. When it was our turn to scan our products, things went fairly smooth. That is, until Spork wanted to do price checks for everything because her items had 99 cent stickers covering up the old prices.

I said, "Spork, you know a pack of hamburger meat is at least $2.00."

She responded, "Yeah, well, that's way too much to pay, so I bring my own stickers and give stuff the price I think it should cost. It's almost like bringing my own coupons and putting what I buy on sale."

"You do know that is also stealing?" I asked.

"No, it isn't. I actually pay for the stuff."

"Spork, it's stealing. When you change the price, you cheat the store out of money, and that's stealing. I'll call over to security and they can explain —"

"That won't be necessary, Wrinkles. Can we split the bill?"

"Yeah, sure, we can split it."

She smiled at me. "Thanks, Wrinkles, that's very nice of you."

I replied, "On one condition."

"What?" asked Spork.

"You slow down and drive the speed limit."

"But my customers —"

"Spork, it's too late."

"But my advertising —"

"Spork, they will know who you are when they see you. Trust me on that."

Spork agreed, so we paid the real prices, bagged up our groceries, and went to the ice cream truck. Spork drove a lot slower on the way back to the school, just like she promised.

During the drive back I asked, "So, you want to own your own restaurant?"

"Oh Wrinkles, I'd love to. All I have to do is find the right people to enjoy my cooking. I'm going to call it *Spork's Stuff* because people will leave my place stuffed from the stuff they eat. I was thinking I could start by feeding hungry college students, kids who forgot their lunches at home, and people who are starving because —"

I politely interrupted, "Perhaps you could find the right food for the right people."

"I never thought of it like that," said Spork.

I had to admit, she was trying. Too bad she had no chance against me.

CHAPTER 35

The Restaurant

While Spork and I were gone, Urhiness and Lenny got along fine. Lenny learned that Urhiness was such a good person, he had nothing bad to say about her. In no time, Lenny realized that Urhiness was like the great, great, great granddaughter he never had. She'd ask his opinion on how well the dishes came out and would even take the small criticisms he gave, if there was need for improvement. For once, Lenny felt involved.

By the time Spork and I climbed up to our classroom, the kitchen looked like a real kitchen and the rest of the room was decorated like a real restaurant. There were place mats made out of laminated paper and Urhiness had organized everything like it was her makeup case. Every one of the pots, pans, dishes, and utensils had a place. Some of them were stored in the cabinets and in easy-to-reach places in the kitchen. Others were hanging from the ceiling like they do on some cooking shows. The two of them had managed to really spruce the place up.

After taking a few steps into our redecorated classroom, I couldn't help but notice that Lenny had on a tuxedo, and from the looks of it, Urhiness had given him a quick makeover. Lenny had a big smile on his face and was helping us with the groceries. While escorting us to the kitchen, Lenny stuck his foot out, and I thought he was trying to trip one of us. Instead, he pointed to a wet spot on the floor, warning us not to slip and fall. This was a Lenny I could get used to having around.

When we made it into the kitchen, Urhiness walked out of the blue bathroom door wearing a beautiful floral dress. She had ditched the flip flops and crown for some comfortable ballet shoes and a ponytail. She had even put some clear fingernail polish on her fingertips. She started dusting the room and shining the silverware to keep from looking in her real mirror. I had to give her credit because she really was trying.

The sound coming from Snooze's desk let us know that he was still snoozing. Now he was dripping wet and looked like he was carrying some extra weight. I think some of the water from the towel was starting to collect inside of the pajamas and he was becoming a human water balloon. Snooze snored out, "Water you looking at?" and continued dreaming. I wasn't quite sure if he was asking me a question, or telling me what my eyes could already see.

It was nearly ten o'clock and dinner needed to be served in roughly two hours. The only way we were going to make it is if we worked together. All we had to do was get started with the cooking and figure out how to wake Snooze.

"Spork, you want to team up and try to get this done together?" I asked.

"You're the opposition," she said. "Wrinkles, we cannot work together. Besides, you'd be trying to steal my recipes to open up a dollar store restaurant and be my competition."

"Well, we need to think of something, so we don't end up serving a late dinner with a side of fifth grade all over again," I said.

"If you let me use that chick of yours, then we'll be working together," replied Spork with a glow in her eyes.

"Never! You know this chick is how I'm going to pass!"

"Look at yourselves," said Urhiness. "Both of you keep arguing back and forth like spoiled brats. Spork, I'll work with you, and we'll work on getting you that restaurant. Wrinkles, Lenny would be honored to work with you."

Lenny added, "Boys rule and Girls drool —"

Urhiness cleared her throat.

Lenny continued, "Girls drool if they leave a little bit of the corner of their mouth open and they have too much saliva in there while they're sleeping."

"You're absolutely right," said Urhiness. "We don't mind you telling the truth, as long as you're not trying to hurt somebody's feelings." She squeezed his cheeks and Lenny actually started blushing.

CHAPTER 36

The Cooking

We split up into two groups and started making the meal. I was in a rush because something told me that Mr. Quiet would be up at midnight and we'd be Spork-made toast. Plus, I had to hurry up and make my food, so I could keep an eye on my chick.

Lenny and I started making That Stuff for dessert. I poured all of the ingredients into a mixing bowl and used the blender to mix it all together. When I finally finished I noticed that it was kind of lumpy, but licking the mixer's beaters let me know it tasted like delicious cream cheese custard. I had Lenny put the mixture into cups and then he put them in the freezer so we could begin making lasagna.

During our food fixing, Lenny couldn't keep his mouth closed. He told me about how Urhiness got her mirror with a free subscription to a magazine when she was four and has been carrying it with her ever since. From what I know about that magazine, it's a doozie. Let's just say it is so horrible for girls, my Grandma Wilbur wouldn't even let Clumsy look at the cover.

Lenny continued to tell me about how Urhiness always saw the people on television looking in the mirror and she figured it was the "in" thing to do. Somehow, she got so hooked on the mirror, she had a hard time getting away from it. Apparently, Lenny tried to help her with the issue, and, in turn, she talked to him about how to treat people better. Things seemed to be better than they were before Spork and I left for the grocery store.

In the meantime, Urhiness was explaining to Spork about layering their version of the dessert like you would put on an outfit. She wanted it to not only taste good, but look good as well. They crushed up the graham crackers and added melted butter to make it easier to cover the bottom of the container.

Urhiness explained, "It's like putting lotion on your body to prevent it from being dry and cracked."

Then, Urhiness talked Spork into mixing the powdered sugar with the cream cheese and putting it on top of the crushed graham crackers. She mentioned something about them complimenting each other like a nice, sweet perfume. Next, they cut up the bananas and strawberries and placed them on top of the cream cheese mixture. The fruit acted as the accessories, like earrings and necklaces. Then they smeared the whipped cream on top of the fruit like a shawl and added the maraschino cherries on top like makeup. It took them about fifteen more minutes than it took us, but their layered creation seemed pretty nice, if you're into fashion. Maybe Urhiness did have a future in design.

The method of my madness for the lasagna was to put all the ingredients into a large roasting pan, and then get the pan into the oven as soon as possible. Lenny and I put the uncooked noodles, raw meats, cheese, and sauce into the pan and slid it in the oven. I closed the door of the oven with my foot and felt pretty good about what we had created. We had saved plenty of time and were just about ready to get started on making the soup.

Our competition didn't take the easy road while preparing their lasagna. They actually took the time to cook all of the meat, except for the pepperoni. Spork grabbed two huge pots that were hanging from the ceiling and used them to boil the noodles and warm up the tomato sauce. Then they added the turkey sausage and ground beef to the tomato sauce to let them mingle and simmer. Next, they put layers of lasagna noodles at the bottom of the pan and spooned the meaty sauce on top of the noodles. A blanket of shredded cheese was sprinkled on top of the meaty sauce and the pieces of pepperoni were carefully placed on top of the cheesy blanket. Spork and Urhiness repeated their process with another layer to make sure their lasagna was extra good. On top of the last blanket of cheese, Spork made a happy face out of the pepperoni and told Urhiness that it looked just like her.

Compared to what Lenny and I had done, it seemed like they were cooking the meal twice. To me, they were wasting time. To Spork and Urhiness, they were double-cooking to make sure their meal was twice as good as their competition. Spork covered her lasagna creation with aluminum foil, slid it in the oven next to mine, and pressed the cooking timer on the oven.

I realized our competition was ready to start their soup when I felt Spork trying to unhook my fanny pack to get to my chick.

"It's allergic to starch!" I shouted. Spork was getting on my nerves.

"Spork, you're allergic to starch?" asked Urhiness.

"Nope," said Spork. "Wrinkles wanted me to believe that the chick he has in his fanny pack is allergic to starch."

"Wrinkles, are you being honest?" asked Lenny.

"No!" I answered coldly.

"Then we should cook it!" shouted Spork, as if I was a dinner party pooper.

"We bought chicken for the soup," I said.

Spork snapped, "But that's fresh chicken right there and I bet it's plump and juicy!"

"My chick isn't even a day old, so there's no way it could be plump and juicy."

Spork reached again and I turned and ran. She chased me around the classroom. We finally ended up on opposite sides of our dining table. When she went left, I moved left too, that way I always kept the same distance between us. Really, our chicken chase could have taken all night.

Just then Lenny wheeled in our direction with a platter in his hand that had a silver cover on top. "Juicy chicken is served."

Lenny took the top off of the platter and showed us what appeared to be a rubber chicken. When I motioned like I was going to grab Lenny's chicken, Spork dove on the table and snatched the rubber chicken off the platter by its neck.

"It's mine!" screamed Spork.

"No, my chick needs a playmate, so it won't get lonely."

"They can both fly the coup and play in my soup!"

"Fine, you keep that chicken and I'll keep mine."

We nodded what could be thought of as a truce and

went back to our cooking stations, so we could continue making the soup.

For my soup, I wanted to do something quick and easy. I didn't bother buying fancy spaghetti noodles. Instead, I bought some Quick Noodles and planned to sprinkle two huge packets of chicken flavor into the boiling water to make the soup taste great. After mixing in my no-so-secret noodle ingredients, I cut up tiny pieces of chicken and added them to my bubbling broth. Finally, I put the lid on the pot.

The so-called opposition actually boiled their chicken first. They even put the real and rubber chicken in the same pot. Then they boiled their fancy spaghetti noodles and heated up the chicken broth. Eventually, they combined all three ingredients into one pot and let it simmer. Dinner would be served soon.

CHAPTER 37

The Beep

When both groups were finished cooking, we sat down at the table and waited for the dessert to cool and the lasagna to cook. The amazing aroma of the food was dancing in and out of our noses. For a few minutes we just sat and relaxed. That's when I saw Snooze out of the corner of my eye.

Instantly, I leaned forward and asked the other three at the table the magic question, "What are we going to do about him?"

"I have no clue," said Lenny. "I had Urhiness count sheep down from one hundred and that didn't even wake him up. We tried to take off his sleeping mask, but it wouldn't budge. I used the water from the towel to get him as wet as I could, but hot and cold water didn't even bother him, either. Personally, I was hoping the water might make him wake up and have to use the bathroom, but that didn't happen."

I said, "We could have Urhiness put makeup on his eyes. Then, I can try to trick him into sleepwalking around, like I did to get him over to the restaurant."

Urhiness replied, "He has to be awake in order to pass. Wrinkles, we have to do this the right way, or he will fail."

Spork pointed at me with her spatula and said, "If Wrinkles would have let me pluck the feathers off that chick of his, we could be using them to tickle Snooze right now."

"Absolutely not," said Urhiness.

Spork shrugged and replied, "It was just a suggestion. We could also put Snooze in a bucket of crabs and then try to yank him out. Those crabs will pinch him and that would most certainly wake him up."

Urhiness giggled and said, "The closest thing to a crab that we have is Crabby Lenny, and he's becoming more like imitation crab meat by the minute."

"Hey now, there's a limitation to my imitation," replied Lenny with a sly grin on his face.

We looked at him and smiled. He really *was* trying.

For the next few minutes, everyone bounced around ideas for waking Snooze. Some included yelling, jump-starting Snooze with some batteries, pulling out his hair one strand at a time, and a bunch of other stuff that was turned down for one reason or another. We had finally decided to start putting ice down his back when the timer let us know the lasagna was finished.

Beep! Beep! Beep!

Mr. Quiet started moving under his sleeping bag, so I walked over to make sure he stayed in dream land. I figured someone had to whisper that it wasn't time to wake up, if his eyes opened. Meanwhile, Spork walked over to the oven, pressed the button to turn off the timer's noise, and took her lasagna out of the oven. By the time she made it back to her seat, I heard the alarm go off again. I hurried over to the oven and also pressed the button to turn the timer off, but that didn't silence the sound. In fact, the sound of the beep got even louder.

BEEP! BEEP! BEEP!

Oh man, Mr. Quiet was moving again and had to be on the verge of waking up.

BEEP! BEEP! BEEP!

I had begun to accept the fact that Mr. Quiet was going to emerge from his hibernation when the beeping suddenly stopped.

CHAPTER 38

The Snooze

At exactly 12:01 a.m., it became obvious that the second series of beeps weren't from the oven. Nope, those loud beeps were actually coming from Snooze's alarm clock on his watch. From the oven area, I watched as Snooze came to life like a moth hatching out of a cocoon. He took off his sleeping mask and began trying to slowly wrestle his way out of the desk that wasn't ready to let him go. When Snooze finally won, the desk fell to the floor in despicable defeat.

As with most people who wake up, Snooze began rubbing his eyes to try to get them to adjust to the light in the room. In a gravelly morning voice he asked, "Hey, where am I? Where am I?"

Maybe he thought he was lost. Maybe he had amnesia. Maybe he had just woken up from a coma.

Before I could answer, Snooze reached for his ribs and winced. "What happened to my ribs? Why do they feel so tender?"

"It's a long story," I said.

"Who are you?" He looked around. "Who are y'all? What's that smell?"

While we all wanted to fill him in on the details, he continued asking questions until he was out of breath. He finally ended with an introduction of sorts.

"My real name is Uncle Bubba. My first name is Uncle and my last name is Bubba. For some reason my friends all call me, 'Snooze,' and I'm okay with that. I'm nocturnal, if you know what that means. For those who don't, I sleep during the day and stay up at night. I've been this way since birth. Y'all look friendly, so you might as well call me Snooze, too."

There were three "Hey, Snooze" replies.

Lenny said, "Hello, Bubba."

"Snooze," snapped Snooze.

"Bubba."

"Snooze."

"Buh-Buh!"

"Meany!"

"Duh! I don't know you! I'm a stranger! Don't talk to strangers!"

"Lenny, Snooze is just trying to be your friend," said Urhiness.

Lenny finally gave in. Nodding, he said, "Hey, Snooze."

After the brief misunderstanding, I introduced Snooze to everybody and caught him up with the details of the day. I told him about his heroic human shield helping at Laura's, and his game-winning catch at the dodgeball game. I thought he would be excited, but he acted like it was no big deal.

"I do that type of stuff in my sleep all the time," he said. "I've learned that the best action happens during the day, while I'm asleep, so I end up doing whatever it takes to get tired again while I am awake." Snooze started running in place to drain his energy.

"Well, keep running because you need to work up an appetite," I said.

Spork, added, "Yeah, we cooked for you."

Snooze nodded and smiled. He had no idea what he was in for. Half of the food he was going to try to eat would probably end up eating him. I knew my creation was at least edible. Spork's mess was sure to have us calling poison control or sending him to the emergency room to have his stomach pumped. I kind of felt sorry for Snooze until I realized that all of us would be going to the hospital because we all had to eat Spork's cooking.

CHAPTER 39

The Brownies

As we all sat and watched Snooze jog in place, I did my best to try to ignore the steam that looked like it was coming off his forehead. I figured his movements were causing the water, still left in his pajamas, to boil. Those thoughts quickly evaporated when the smoke detector suddenly went off. I ran to it and started fanning it with a dish rag to help move the smoky air away, to stop yet another alarm from beeping. Urhiness opened a window to let out some of the smoke and Snooze ended up taking my towel to keep working up his appetite.

"Just take the batteries out," said Lenny.

I replied, "We can't do that. What happens if there really is smoke in here in the future?"

Lenny answered, "Look, I'm just trying to solve the problem, and right now, our problem is that Mr. Quiet could wake up." He pointed at Mr. Quiet who was rustling under his sleeping bag again.

Urhiness added, "Mr. Quiet won't wake up if you get a towel and help us!"

With Lenny and Snooze using the helicopter-style towel twirling to get a great deal of the smoke away from the detector and out of the kitchen area, I was able to see exactly where the smoke was coming from. I quickly made my way over to the oven and remembered what I had forgotten to do.

When I opened up the oven door, black smoke started rolling out and into the air. I quickly made my hands dive into some oven mitts, lifted my lasagna out of the oven, and placed the roasting pan on top of the stove. It didn't take much inhaling to discover that the burnt smell of *my* lasagna had a stench like no other. It was sizzling and there was a small fire in the middle. My main course was being char-broiled right in front of my eyes.

By the time I waved the oven mitts enough to put the fire out, I overhead Snooze whispering to Lenny, "Brownies, man, I love brownies."

Lenny said, "I don't —"

Snooze interrupted, "You don't have to like them. I'll eat the entire pan."

Lenny replied, "You probably don't want to eat that, Snooze."

Snooze smiled and continued to help Lenny with the smoke. Those two had managed to get enough smoke out of the room to stop the smoke detector from beeping, allowing Urhiness to close the window. Meanwhile, I ended up grabbing a package of sliced American cheese out of the refrigerator. Even though that type of cheese was not on the ingredients list, and I wasn't sure if anything I found in Spork's refrigerator was safe, I didn't have time to be picky. I started placing the pieces of cheese on top of the burnt lasagna to create an extra cheesy roof of melted yellow to my dish. At that point, it was looking better, but honestly, I didn't think for a minute that it could possibly taste great.

By the time I put the last slice of cheese on my lasagna, Snooze and Lenny had joined me by the oven. Snooze said, "It almost looks like Wrinkles is putting some slices of lemon frosting on the top to make it taste extra good."

Before I could say anything, Lenny handed Snooze and me some sport coats and ties to wear.

"What's this for?" I asked, with intentions on getting a real answer.

"You want honesty?" replied Lenny.

"Sure."

"Wrinkles, you look like a bag of smashed apples and you need to wear something that shows you respect a fancy restaurant like this."

"Lenny, this is a classroom, not a fancy restaurant."

"Fine, you go over there and tell Urhiness that this place isn't a fancy restaurant."

"Okay, maybe you're right," I agreed.

Lenny replied, "I know I'm right, so take my advice when I tell you that the wool sweater, those spandex shorts, and the championship fanny pack will not give you the dignified look you need in order to dine at this establishment."

I gave Lenny's words some food for thought and replied, "I'll wear the sport coat, but I'm not wearing the tie because I'm not wearing a shirt with a collar."

Lenny handed one sport coat to me and gave the other to Snooze. Snooze wore his over his shoulders and returned to jogging while Lenny escorted us back to the table. Lenny pulled out our seats and we sat down quickly, before he could go back to his old ways of pulling them out from under us, so we would hit the ground.

Snooze unfolded his napkin and put it in his lap. Spork, Lenny, and I followed his lead and did the same with our napkins.

Urhiness walked over from the window area, put our paper menus on the table in front of us, and nervously asked, "Is there anything I can get you for starters?"

I could tell she was still getting used to looking at something other than her mirror, but I was proud of the fact that she was indeed making progress. I took a minute to look over the menu that only had the selections we were allowed to make and laughed to myself. Snooze, who had been asleep and didn't witness what we went through to prepare the meals, was studying the menu with a focused face.

He finally broke the silence at the table by asking, "How is the chicken noodle soup?"

Spork answered, "Some chickens think it's to die for."

I smiled at her and patted my fanny pack.

From there, Snooze ordered one of everything. Lenny, Spork, and I decided to have what Snooze was having. Urhiness wrote everything down and went away to grab the first course.

Snooze leaned over to Lenny and whispered, "I didn't see the brownies that Wrinkles made on the menu. Maybe they'll be a special, surprise dessert that we get before we leave."

"Those *brownies* were on the menu," answered Lenny.

CHAPTER 40

The Eating

The first course of our dinner was, of course, the chicken noodle soup. There were two steaming hot pots set in front of us. I could very obviously tell the difference between the two soups because Spork's pot had a rubber chicken head sticking out of it. The beady little eyes of the rubber chicken seemed to stare at everybody in the room and watch our every move. I had to turn away because all I could think of at a time like this was my own chick.

Snooze, on the other hand, was all about getting the rubber chicken before anyone else did. He picked up the hot pot and started pouring the contents into his open mouth. The scalding, hot soup was burning his tongue and the roof of his mouth when Lenny pulled the soup away from him.

"Bubba, at a restaurant like this, you need to put your soup in a bowl and use a spoon to eat with," said Lenny.

"I'm hungry and I can't wait that long! Besides, I didn't let the side of the pot touch my mouth to get my germs."

"We still can't eat like that in a restaurant like this," replied Lenny.

"Well, I'm not trying to let anyone beat me to the good soup. That other bowl right there doesn't even have bubble gum chicken in it, like this one. If it doesn't have bubble gum chicken in it, then I don't want it." He pointed to the rubber chicken and continued, "And I cannot get that entire piece of bubble gum into a small soup bowl."

Lenny said, "Bubba, I'll take care of it."

Then, Lenny whipped out a pair of scissors, and cut the head off the rubber chicken. Once again, I couldn't stand to watch. Lenny gave the head of the rubber chicken to Snooze, as a souvenir. Then Lenny used a larger bowl to stretch the remainder of the rubber chicken around the perimeter of bowl so it would look like a plastic bag in a garbage can. Lenny poured some soup into the rubber chicken and gave the new holding container to Snooze. Snooze picked up the bowl and started slurping out the soup, one long inhale at a time. Then Lenny served everyone else at the table in regular bowls. The other three soup sippers ate just as quickly as Spork. I only had a spoonful because I didn't want to risk getting sick.

When it was time for us to eat my soup, I brightened up. Snooze must have followed my lead with Spork's soup because he only took one spoonful and then started chewing on the head of the rubber chicken. Maybe if I hadn't gone the Quick-Noodle-with-minimal-real-chicken route, Snooze would have eaten more. When I tried my own soup, I quickly decided to save room for the lasagna and dessert.

After Lenny took the soups away, he brought over the main course. I pretty much knew my lasagna was not going to be the better of the two because of the four alarm fire and third degree burn issues that I covered up with the cheese. My only hope of beating Spork was her reputation of messing up some good eating by going crazy with the ingredients.

With my lasagna now smoldering and on the table, Lenny pulled out a hammer and chisel to help cut and scoop what looked to be charcoal briquettes covered in cheese.

"Brownies with lemon frosting are my favorite," said Snooze.

"Wrinkles enjoys them, too," replied Lenny under his breath, while I thought about giving this burnt brownie to a dog to gnaw on a like a rawhide bone.

Watching Snooze attempt to enjoy my lasagna actually disturbed me. He tried to use the side of the fork to slide through the meat, noodles, and cheese, but he ended up bending his fork. Then he reached for his knife and had to hacksaw his way through the cheese-covered brick. When he did bite into a crunchy piece of the burnt lasagna flavored jaw breaker he said, "Are these crunchy things macadamia nuts or toffee?"

"Neither," I said.

"Oh, it's a secret oven-roasted ingredient?"

I used taking a bite of my own lasagna medicine as an excuse to not answer Snooze's question. I had food in my mouth, and to be honest, the lasagna was nastier than burnt popcorn and bacon. Instantly, my very best taste buds decided that we weren't friends anymore. At that point, nobody else at the table was willing to torture their tongues by eating anymore of my lasagna. Lenny removed my lasagna from the table and Urhiness uncovered Spork's creation.

One look at Spork's cheesy delight had us hardly able to contain ourselves. The lasagna's hypnotizing scent had all five of us moving like charmed cobras. Even the pepperoni smile had us thinking the lasagna was actually happy to see us. As Lenny began dishing out one plentiful piece after another, the melted strings of cheese looked like bridges that connected the lasagna on the plate to the container it was cooked in.

As Lenny was deciding who would get the first piece of Spork's lasagna, we all almost started sword-fighting with our knives to claim it. Before any metal could clang though, we put those measly weapons back on the table and picked up our forks. Instead of trying to claim the piece Lenny had, we all started eating directly out of the pan. Not a word was said as the five of us grunted, groaned, mmm-ed, burped, and made room for more.

When I, of all people, threw in the final fork, the only remaining piece was what would be considered the nose of the happy face.

"I could see myself eating that often," said Urhiness.

"Yeah, that was the best lasagna ever," added Lenny.

Spork smiled and we all managed to sit quietly at the table so our stomachs could do the talking for us. Clearly, we had eaten so much lasagna, we hadn't even considered leaving room for dessert, but the sound of Mr. Quiet moving under his sleeping bag served as motivation for us to get to the last course of the meal.

Since all of us were so stuffed full of lasagna that nobody could get out of their chairs to get the dessert, we had to do the next best thing. Urhiness reached behind her and grabbed a bag of jump ropes. We untangled them and tied one jump rope to more jump ropes until we had a huge jump rope. We lassoed one of the jump ropes around Lenny's shoulders and pushed him into the kitchen to get the desserts. Lenny ended up stopping by crashing into the refrigerator door. He screamed in agony and we realized that his scream meant that he was actually regaining some feeling in his legs.

After opening the refrigerator door and putting the delicious desserts on his lap, Lenny said, "Whoa, these things are cold."

"But are they good and cold?" asked Snooze.

"Reel me back in and you'll find out!"

Snooze tried to reel Lenny back like a human yoyo, but the jump ropes and the chair only moved a few inches. I joined Snooze's effort by grabbing the rope, and we began to have a tug of war with Lenny's wheelchair, because none of us noticed that one of the front tires was blocked by something that wouldn't allow the wheelchair to go in reverse.

"Pull harder, guys, or I'll be stuck over here until my food digests!" said Lenny.

We counted to three and yanked the rope with enough force to get the job done. The only problem was that before we yanked the rope, it slid down below Lenny's shoulders and rested around his stomach. We continued to pull without paying any attention to the fact that Lenny was getting dragged to the table with his fully-loaded stomach being squeezed by the jump rope. In between tugs, we could hear Lenny saying what sounded like, "You're about to make me slow up!" We kept snatching the rope with more force because we didn't want him to slow up. I mean, we had to show him that we were capable of getting him back to the table with the dessert.

By the time we finally reeled Lenny in, we realized that the rope was extra tight on his stomach and he was actually saying, "You're about to make me throw up."

While Lenny's face was filled with fury and his eyes were watering, the desserts were still intact when they were delivered to the table. I loosened the jump rope from around him and he tried to rub plenty of pain away from his stomach. Snooze took the desserts off his lap and gave them to Urhiness, who used a real spatula to scoop Spork's creation out of the container and onto small saucers. Then, she used an ice cream scoop to spoon my dessert out of the cups, and place it into small bowls.

After looking at both versions of the dessert resting in front of me, I realized that Spork's version looked better than mine. The layered effect they used allowed us to see what we were eating before we used our spoons to make it disappear. My version of the dessert had the look of delicious, fruity ice cream with chunks of graham crackers blended inside.

When I went to slide my spoon into my dessert, Lenny said, "Ladies first."

I pushed my dessert bowl back and allowed my spoon to slide effortlessly to the bottom of Spork's dessert in order to collect some of the graham cracker foundation. I lifted the spoon to my mouth and the first taste made my eyes roll into the back of my head. It was so good, I dropped my spoon and buried my face in the dish. After I devoured the entire dessert, I licked my lips and looked at everyone else. They were licking their plates clean, so I decided to follow their lead.

When each of us tasted a spoonful of my dessert and decided we were too full to eat anymore, we all seemed to agree that dinner was over. While everyone else sat back in their chairs and relaxed, I began writing my article for the Old Endings Observer.

CHAPTER 41

The Quiet

Maybe we had been too busy eating like squirrels to notice Mr. Quiet watching our every move.

He interrupted our silence by saying, "I can't believe you all used those terrible table manners at a fine dining establishment like this."

Spork replied, "Mr. Quiet, if you knew how good this food was, you would have done the same thing."

"Spork, I guess that means that you failed because if Wrinkles' food was that good, then I cannot imagine you beating him."

I chimed in, "You're wrong, Mr. Quiet. My dessert is right there and it wasn't as good as Spork's."

Mr. Quiet pointed to my dessert and responded, "The one that I've always had looks just like that."

"I'll have you know," said Urhiness while looking Mr. Quiet in the eyes, "Not only did Spork out-cook Wrinkles with dessert, but her other two creations were far superior to what the competition brought to the table."

"Is this true, Lenny?" asked Mr. Quiet. He was fully intending to have Lenny blast Spork's cooking with enough information to allow Mr. Quiet to fail both her and him at the same time.

Lenny answered, "Well, to be honest, Spork did out-prepare and out-cook Wrinkles. Wrinkles' cooking displayed typical household cooking. You know how it is when parents rush through cooking and use whatever is in the refrigerator to get the job done. All the while, the television and video games watch the kids. Wrinkles' soup was for the sick, and not the sophisticated. His lasagna had neglect written all over it in the form of third degree burns. How many homes have cooks who burn food because they forget to check their food?"

"So, let me get this straight," said Mr. Quiet. "Wrinkles only burned his lasagna and Spork's still tasted better?"

"Yes!" answered Lenny. He continued, "Mr. Quiet, while the desserts were both good, Spork went the extra mile in appearance and preparation to make a dessert that is better than birthday cake. And, I should know, because when you get to be my age, you've sampled a lot of birthday cakes."

Mr. Quiet looked shocked. He couldn't remember the last time Lenny had said several sentences in a row without insulting someone else. He had never known Spork to cook anything that was plate-licking good. He had never looked Urhiness in the eye. He had never seen Snooze awake. All of these shocking events were starting to confuse him.

Mr. Quiet added, "I must be dreaming."

When Mr. Quiet turned and walked back to his sleeping area to get more rest, Snooze jogged over to him and shook Mr. Quiet's shoulder.

"What now? Can't you see I'm trying to sleep?" asked Mr. Quiet.

"Look, I heard you say that you were dreaming and I'm just letting you know that you're awake."

"I can't be asleep if you're going to shake my shoulder and wake me up."

"Sorry about that. It's just that you're the first real teacher I ever remember seeing. I always dreamed about teachers being older and bigger, but I guess this is pretty cool. What's your name?"

"Mr. Quiet."

"Do you want me to whisper? Am I talking too loud?" asked Snooze.

"No, my name is Mr. Quiet. Snooze, why haven't you ever met your teachers?"

"Well, I was born nocturnal. On school nights, I was always up late playing video games and watching television. The only reason I set my alarm in the morning was to let me know when I had to turn the television off and get ready for school. Since my parents had to drop me off early, I'd go into my classroom and fall asleep before anyone else would get there. I'd sleep through the entire school day and evening. When I finally would wake up, I'd get my homework and go home."

"I see," said Mr. Quiet, with a confused look on his face. "Snooze, you do know that you need to stay up for the rest of the night in order to pass the fifth grade?"

"Oh, I'll be up because I don't start getting tired until about 7:00 a.m. Then I turn off like I have a light switch on my back."

"Well, you better not go to sleep before seven o'clock, or you'll fail."

"So, what do the others have to do to pass?" asked Snooze.

Mr. Quiet paused for a second before he sat up to look at the rest of us. He gave us that crazy smile of his and said, "They have already failed. They'll be back tomorrow and probably every other night for the rest of their lives."

CHAPTER 42

The Reverse

According to Mr. Quiet, we failed. Failed! We would be back tomorrow and probably every other night for the rest of our lives! With those words, the air left the room. The five of us had done everything it took to pass and it wasn't going to be enough. Mr. Quiet was playing dirty again, but I had a strange feeling he was testing us. I remained as calm as I could, and looked at the others, because this wasn't a time to panic. We all gave Mr. Quiet our own teeth-showing smiles and his quickly melted away.

Lenny interrupted the silence by saying, "Well, if you need us to sit with you tomorrow, we would be more than happy to do that."

"I don't need a baby sitter," said Mr. Quiet with a bitter tone.

"I don't mind keeping more than one eye on you," said Urhiness with a loving glow. She continued, "Besides, I could use the extra money for college."

"You have to pass fifth grade before you get to college, Miss Mirror."

"Did you just call me Miss Mirror?"

"I sure did," answered Mr. Quiet.

"Maybe you're right. Maybe I will miss the mirror, but I am letting it go."

To all of our surprise, Urhiness walked up to Mr. Quiet and handed him her broken mirror with a bright blue bow wrapped around it. That gift to him immediately showed us that her subscription to her magazine was finally cancelled!

"Urhiness," said Spork. "I don't mind coming over while you babysit Mr. Quiet. I'll stop by around midnight and bring some warm milk. I'll even make cookies, brownies, Brussels sprouts, fish sticks, or a Shark Knuckle Omelet without egg shells."

"I DON'T LIKE BRUSSELS SPROUTS AND I DON'T NEED A BABY SITTER!"

"Okay, you don't have to eat the Brussels sprouts."

Snooze offered his help to Urhiness by saying, "If Mr. Quiet needs somebody to play with when he wakes up, call me. We can even build forts and play flashlight tag."

"I DON'T NEED A BABY SITTER!" screamed Mr. Quiet.

I added, "I don't mind treating you like the chick and taking good care of you. I'll be the kangaroo and you can be the joey. I think my Grandma Wilbur can get me a bigger fanny pack."

"I DON'T NEED A BABY SITTER!"

I continued, "Really, Mr. Quiet, it won't be too much trouble for any of us. Lenny can read you bedtime stories, Spork can get you fed before bed, Urhiness will dress you in some stylish pajamas, Snooze will be there when you want to play hide-and-go-seek, and I'll be responsible for making sure that everything goes just fine."

"I DON'T NEED A BABY SITTER!" Mr. Quiet had started to cry huge elephant-sized tears at that point. He explained, "I need the world to have more people who care about each other. I need to see people who are willing to put aside their differences to work together to be better people. I need to know that people are willing to change their bad habits into good habits. I need for people to learn from their mistakes. I need people who can cook a good meal that will bring people together to eat at one table, instead of spread out all over the place. I need the older generation to care about what the younger generation is doing and share its wisdom. And, most of all, I need —"

He stopped, mid-sentence.

We all paused and looked at each other. He was speaking to us, to everybody in the world, and we understood him.

He continued, "Most of all, I need a tissue!"

By that time, the tears were streaming down his face. He was so caught up in the emotion of the moment that his little nose was running like Snooze's drool. Urhiness fished through her purse and gave him some tissue.

Mr. Quiet blew his nose like a trombone and said, "Today has been a great day at Old Endings Preparatory because all of you have proven that teamwork makes the dream work."

"So, we all passed?" asked Lenny.

"Yes, you passed. Now pack up your things because I have to feed the turtles."

"What about the lion?" asked Spork.

"I'm going to let it gnaw on Wrinkles' leftovers."

"He can have the rest of my brownies," said Snooze.

We all laughed and I asked, "So, now, what do I need to do with this chick?"

CHAPTER 43

The Swipe

"Open the window and put the chick out on the ledge," said Mr. Quiet. "The mother will be waiting for it."

I looked toward the windows and noticed that the sun was up early and yawning, while still hiding behind the morning clouds. On the ledge, the mother hen was looking at my fanny pack with the same beady eyes as the rubber chicken. I walked over to the window and opened it up. I unzipped my fanny pack and nearly had a heart attack.

THE CHICK WAS GONE!

I started reaching around the fanny pack to see if there was some sort of secret compartment the chick may have been hiding in. Nope. I took a deep breath and turned quickly in a circle to see if the chick was by my desk, going to the blue bathroom, or hanging out near the turtles. It wasn't.

"What's wrong?" said Mr. Quiet. He smiled again and I knew what that meant.

"I don't have the baby chick in my fanny pack. I must have —"

I couldn't bring myself to say that I had lost the chick. Suddenly, I was a nervous wreck and sweat started pouring through the sport coat. My mouth was dry and my heart was doing jumping jacks in my chest because I had just failed fifth grade, again.

Spork distracted me from certain doom when she said, "Wrinkles, thank you so much for letting me figure out how the chick for my chicken noodle soup should smell, even if I couldn't use your chick to figure out how my chicken needed to taste."

Spork brought her oven mitt from behind her back and showed me exactly where my baby chick was resting. She winked, joined me by the window, and handed me the chirping chick. Before Mr. Quiet could start asking questions, Lenny gave him a recap of the events.

As I placed the baby chick out on the ledge, I whispered to Spork, "When did you take it?"

"When you were eating my lasagna like a greedy goblin, I managed to get it out of the fanny pack."

"The alarm on the fanny pack didn't even go off."

"I have my ways of getting around alarms. My plan was to add some of the feathers to my dessert, but I realized that it didn't need anything else to be delicious, because I had the right food for the people. So for the rest of the meal, I just held her and made sure she had sunflower seeds to eat because she was hungry."

"Well, thanks for taking care of her, and not plucking her to death."

As Spork and I talked, the mother bird walked the baby chick down the ledge and we could hear the two of them talking about the events of their night. Spork and I joined the others, just as Lenny was finishing up the summary of the day.

Mr. Quiet said, "Congratulations! I made these last week."

After Mr. Quiet gave each of us a certificate and diploma for passing 5th grade, Urhiness thanked each of us for helping her find a new outlook on life. Spork told us that we were all promised a job at the new restaurant she would be opening very soon. Snooze yawned and told us that if we made it to twenty-two thousand while counting sheep, we could call him. Lenny seemed to be a little unhappy about leaving his home until Mr. Quiet gave him the telephone number for Agnes, the greeter I met at the grocery store. He hopped out of his wheelchair, jumped in the air, did a little shuffle, and slid down the pole. I looked out the window and saw him sprinting toward Garden-Gotten Foods.

After saying goodbye to everyone, I slid down the pole. I walked out of the building, passed students on their way into the school, and toward my Grandma Wilbur's motorcycle. I was too deep in thought to hear the lion's roar after the tardy bell rang. I didn't even notice the music coming from Spork's ice cream truck.

I picked up my helmet, flashed my finest crooked-tooth smile to my Grandma Wilbur, and climbed on the back of her motorcycle. While we zoomed away from Old Endings Preparatory, I looked at that polka-dot building and realized I had learned a lot during my day and night there. I made some cool friends who were diverse, but not divisible. I became more responsible for my own actions and realized that teamwork really had made our dreams work. As the view of the school faded away from my eyes, I thought to myself, long live Old Endings Preparatory and long live the KNIGHTS OF NIGHT SCHOOL!

Acknowledgements

To my wife and son: I'd like thank you two for allowing me to spend so much time thinking to myself and writing. You always welcomed me out of my world and embraced me with good times. I love both of you more than you'll ever know.

To my parents: Thank you for pushing me to be more and do more. Pops, your work ethic is inspirational. Ma, I'm still trying to be a bigger return on your investment. Miss C., I know you're always talking to Him for me.

To my extended family: Our reunions on the phone and in person always make me feel great about being a member of a wonderful group of people.

To my writing partners: Danielle and Matt, I appreciate you for reading everything I write and asking important questions that keep me being true to the characters, the stories, the writing, and to myself.

To my EMU graduate panel: All of the dissecting of my art and challenging me to defend my thoughts, or make changes, helped me to make this book stronger.

To my teachers: Thank you for taking the time to get to know me.

To all of my uncles and brothers: We always share humor, life, and experiences. My talent is a mere portion of our talents!

To the educators who allowed this book to be a part of your busy lives: The feedback you gave kept me wanting to improve my writing. Allowing my book to be in your classrooms was an honor.

To the Eastern Michigan Writing Project, Class of 2011: Our month together was a blessing that fast-forwarded my transition to becoming a writer. Having your seal of approval has done wonders for my sacred writing life.

To my Meridia family: I cannot thank you enough for believing in my talent, listening to my goals, and helping me to get this project out to the world. This has been a wonderful journey!

Finally, to all the students I have worked with over the years: What we have shared in the classroom has been amazing. I write books for you, and I realize I could not have written them without you.

Steady,

MARQUIN

CPSIA information can be obtained at www.ICGtesting.com
Printed in the USA
LVOW131938120313

323919LV00001B/1/P